# THE GHOST OF CHRISTMAS ALWAYS

# THE GHOST OF CHRISTMAS ALWAYS

*includes the original Charles Dickens classic,*
*A Christmas Carol*

## KEVIN J. ANDERSON

## CHARLES DICKENS

WFP

WordFire Press

# CONTENTS

# INTRODUCTION

## KEVIN J. ANDERSON

Early in my career as a writer, my annual tradition was to spend the holidays with a group of writer friends, most of whom were clustered around Eugene, Oregon. I lived in the San Francisco Bay Area where I worked as a technical writer for a large research laboratory—in other words, I had a "real job"—but I very much wanted to be a full-time writer and worked at my stories and novels, gradually seeing some success.

Each year I would make the drive up Interstate 5 along the spine of California to Oregon, and in questionable mid-December weather, but I didn't want to miss my holiday gathering. One year I even took my fiancée Rebecca Moesta with me (and she and I just celebrated our 26th wedding anniversary).

One of the Eugene locals would act as the host, and we'd get together the day before Christmas for conversation and cooking. Some people baked cookies or other desserts; I always made my famous lasagna, a masterpiece of a recipe that has been in my family for five generations. (Yes, turkey or ham might be more traditional, but we were a group who broke with traditions—we were writers, after all—and formed our own.)

After the late afternoon feast, we passed out gifts. In keeping with being starving writers, no gift could cost more than a dollar, which forced us to do some imaginative shopping.

After the gift giving, we sat around for the highlight of the evening—the real sharing of gifts among writers, usually by a fireplace, usually with mulled cider. We would take out printed manuscripts, stories that we each had written specially for the occasion, which had never been read before. We went around in a circle, reading aloud one story after another. Some were heartwarming, some were scary, some magical, some imaginative, some haunting. Each of us had our own particular spin on the holiday season.

We were all new writers, learning our craft and learning the business. We poured our hearts and our energies into these stories.

In the years since, members of our group have become international bestselling authors, *New York Times* bestselling authors, winners or nominees of almost every award in numerous genres, from the Writers of the Future Award to the Hugo, Nebula, World Fantasy, Philip K. Dick, Bram Stoker, Shamus, Edgar, Pushcart, Endeavor, Sidewise, Scribe, Locus, Mythopoeic Society, Romantic Times Reviewers' Choice, and Theodore Sturgeon Awards (and probably many others). Some have become publishers themselves, or movie producers, record producers, game designers.

Maybe there was magic in those Christmas Eves after all.

This was a novelette I wrote for that gathering, one of my most heartfelt stories that goes beyond the Christmas spirit to the core of what it means to be a writer.

ix

# THE GHOST OF CHRISTMAS ALWAYS

## KEVIN J. ANDERSON

*"After she died I dreamed of her every night for many months, sometimes as a spirit, sometimes as a living creature, never with any of the bitterness of my real sorrow, but always with a kind of quiet happiness, which became so pleasant to me that I never lay down at night without a hope of the vision coming back … And so it did."*

—Charles Dickens, in a letter to the mother of Mary Hogarth, 1842

STAVE ONE


Mary was dead, to begin with. And yet each Christmas Eve her ghost came to haunt Charles Dickens. He waited the year round for the one night he could see her again, if only for a brief time.

Dickens gripped the arms of his chair, then let his eyes fall half closed. Across from him, aromatic smoke came from a fire in the sitting-room hearth. On the mantelpiece sat a scrolled ivory-and-gold clock with slim hands reaching toward midnight, when Mary would come. Wind rattled the window panes, pushing winter cold into the great house on Devonshire Terrace. The Dickenses had added mahogany doors, marble mantels, and carpets to their new home—such extravagance was expected from the author of *Nicholas Nickleby*, *Oliver Twist*, and of course the *Pickwick Papers*.

But on the silent night before Christmas, the house felt like a deserted stage in the theater, filled with props and costumes but no actors. Mary had never lived here with them. His young sister-in-law had died before the unparalleled success swept over Dickens's life.

He stood up from the chair, brushed at his robe, and walked to the mantel. Dickens had urged the four children, his wife Kate, and the maid to retire early this night. None of them would suspect why he wanted them fast asleep. Beside the clock stood Mary's portrait, painted by Phiz, the artist who illustrated so many of Dickens's installments. After Mary's death had devastated him, Dickens begged Phiz to do the portrait from memory, as a special favor. Now Dickens touched the lines of her face, the soft eyes gazing at something unseen but wondrous, the curves of her dark hair. Sweet Mary Hogarth, the delightful sister of his moody and shallow-minded wife. Kate would be snoring upstairs, grossly pregnant with their fifth child. She would carry out the same chores on Christmas day as she did every day. She had no broader imagination, doing only what she felt her wifely obligations demanded. Not like young Mary, who was always so bright, so fascinated.... "Can't you gaze at that portrait any time, Charles Dickens? I have only a short while here with you."

Dickens turned, smiling. He felt a rush of happiness. Mary Hogarth stood there, spectral and unchanged since her death six years before. She wore a shimmering white gown that reflected a light not from the fireplace and blew in a breeze that Dickens himself could not feel. "I was waiting for you," he said.

"Just as I wait for this one night when I'm allowed to see you again." She took a step forward but did not touch him. She made no sound as she moved. "This year I have a present for you, Charles, a gift I hope you will treasure as much as I treasure giving it to you."

He could not think of what to say. He, Charles Dickens, who spoke in front of great audiences, who played in the theater, who read his own sketches aloud to crowds from the streets, found himself unable to utter a simple sentence to the wavering image of a sixteen-year-old girl. He finally said, "Merely seeing you again is enough to make me glad for the next twelve months." Mary smiled and, keeping her gaze on his, reached forward to touch the clock. "But this is better. I give you Time."

"Time?" he asked, not comprehending but feeling his heart filled with wonder. "I do need more of it, with all my commitments."

"No," she said with a lilt in her voice that reminded him of the times that they laughed, Charles and Kate and Mary, when they went on outings to the theater. "I give you *your* time, Charles. Your past, your present, and what is yet to come."

Before he could say more, Mary turned the hour hand backward from midnight in a full circle until it reached eleven o'clock. As the hand touched the top of the dial, the chimes rang out. Mary extended her fingers to him. "Take my hand, Charles. Let me show you."

Eagerly he wrapped his fingers around her cold flesh, insubstantial but as strong and insistent as the wind. Mary led him to the window and drew back the curtains. The distant lights of London sprawled out below, making him think of the crowded streets, tall buildings leaning out over alleys, small fires and candlelit windows.

"Step with me into the past," she said.

Fighting back the tremors of fear in his voice, Dickens asked, "Long past?"

"No. Your past." And she stepped partway through the window, through the sash as if it were no more than a bit of fog.

"Wait!" he cried, "I am mortal! I cannot pass through brick and stone and glass."

"Bear but a touch of my hand, Charles." As Mary said this, she gave a tug.

Dickens walked forward clad only in slippers and dressing-gown, blinking as he stepped through and out into a clear winter night. But he felt no cold, no wind, only astonishment, for he found himself many miles from his home on Devonshire Terrace.

STAVE TWO

Though it was dark, Dickens could make out the three-storey house before him, with glowing orange lights in several of the windows. By day he would be able to see the nearby Kentish countryside, Chatham, and the Medway Valley.

"Good Heaven!" Dickens cried, "I was a boy here! My father worked in the naval dockyard."

Mary just smiled at him and raised her hand. Dickens found that they floated off the ground, rising along the terraces and shingles, to one of the upstairs windows where a single light still burned.

"That was my room!" Dickens said, keeping his voice to a whisper.

"And here is someone you'll like to see, no doubt."

They pressed their faces close to the window, and Dickens noted that, though the winter air must be very cold, neither his breath nor Mary's left any frost upon the window.

Inside the room he saw a plump woman with grayish-brown hair tied neatly behind her head. She sat in a chair pulled near to a pair of beds in which lay a boy and a girl. Both children had eyes wide and mouths slack with rapt fascination and terror. The woman leaned forward to talk; her eyes squinted and her face contorted as she spoke, waving her hands.

"Why it's old Mary Weller, our maid! Bless her heart—Mary Weller alive again!"

The maid lurched out in the middle of her story, splaying her fingers like claws.

Both children squirmed backward in their beds, defending themselves with nervous giggling.

Dickens, delighted, turned to the spirit beside him. "She used to tell us horrible stories about Captain Murderer! And how he'd indulge his taste in wives by killing them off and baking them into pies! Ugh—my sister Fanny and I used to lie awake shivering in terror every time she told us one of those stories. But I loved them. I used to make up my own."

Mary patted him with her cold hand. "You've been a writer since the time you were a little boy. Come with me, around the corner." They descended to the ground again, but when they turned the corner, Dickens found that they had reached an alley far distant from the old house. The light had changed to a gray wintry afternoon. People crowded the street, women wrapped in dark clothes tugging children alongside them on the frozen mud. Thawed patches of slush surrounded steaming piles of fresh horse manure. Dogs ran about, harrying burly men who carried packages and crates. Off to one side a man hauled a narrow pauper's coffin on his back, passing unnoticed through the streets. Signboards protruded out over doors proclaiming lodging houses, barbers, poulterers, a tripe shop, a sausage-maker.

"This is the Strand!" Dickens said, nearly letting go of

Mary's hand in his excitement. "I got lost here one day when I was a boy."

"In fact, there you are right now." Mary indicated a small child gawking at the crowds, stumbling along with wonder-filled eyes. The boy looked as if he had been crying, but the tears dried to streaks in the cold air. "I had a shilling and fourpence in my pocket," Dickens said. "My godfather gave it to me. I knew I would be rescued somehow. And I was very hungry." They followed the boy, observing yet unseen by the pedestrians. Little Charles Dickens walked along, dressed in a warm jacket, bumping into unshaven men who ignored him. He stared from window to window in food shops, shuffling his feet, looking around. He kept walking. Finally he stopped in front of a pile of cooked sausages in a window. A paper sign in front read, "Small Germans, a Penny." The boy stared at the sausages, shivering. He licked his lips. He took a deep breath, mustering courage, and strode in. The shopkeeper squinted at him with an amused grin, but the boy seemed confident now that he knew what to ask for.

"If you please, would you sell me one of those sausages?" His voice sounded tiny as Dickens listened. The boy reached into his pocket and took out a single penny. The shopkeeper used his fingers to pick up one of the sausages from the back of the pile and plucked the penny from the boy's hand at the exact moment he surrendered the sausage. Charles Dickens felt his cheeks flushing with the delight of the memory. "The sausage wasn't very warm," he told Mary, "but it was one of the most delicious things ever to pass my lips. Of course part of it was that I had bought it myself."

The boy wandered the streets again, in and out of yards and little squares, chased off by cooks he gawked at, bullied by a gang of young toughs who wanted the rest of the money in his pockets. The boy broke into a run, pushing through the crowds, splashing in the slush, until he lost the boys in a dark alley lined with dim counting houses where misers changed their gold.

The boy stood in the growing dark, looking unspeakably forlorn.

"Can we not help him?" Dickens said.

Mary shook her head. "No, Charles, we are here only to observe. You pity this boy now, but would you have traded that single day in your life for anything you can imagine?"

"No, never. It astonishes me even now to think of how much I used from that day in *Oliver Twist*, and in *Nicholas Nickleby*, and in half a dozen of my sketches for the periodicals."

"And you will continue to find ways to use it. You're a writer, Charles, heart and soul. Everything you experience is fodder for the tales that delight so many people."

As Mary spoke, Dickens heard a loud cough and saw a middle-aged man come up to the wretched boy and ask what was wrong. The man's clothes were drab and worn, but the brass buttons on his coat had been polished with care.

"That watchman took me home," Dickens said in a whisper. "I remember his cough, how he wheezed all the way. I was afraid I was going to catch the plague from him."

Mary strolled ahead, turning her back on the departing boy and the coughing watchman. "Why don't you come around the corner with me? We'll pass another decade."

Still astounded, Dickens followed her as the scene once again changed. He found himself in a dark court, narrow but clean. Clouds the color of ice on a deep pond covered the sky. In front of a dark office, a young man strode by with a polished walking stick. He looked like a twenty-year-old dandy, with gleaming shoes, black waistcoat and vest. His gray felt trousers were new and unwrinkled, his green cravat impeccably tied. The brim of a brushed top hat shaded his face. The young man moved with a nervous manner as he stopped in front of the dark office—and then Dickens recognized the mail slot and the stencilled letters above it that read EDITOR'S BOX.

"This is Fleet Street! That's me, posting my very first contribution for the *Monthly Magazine*." The young man pulled out a long envelope and, trying to appear nonchalant, slipped it into the black hole of the mail slot before striding away. He rapped his walking stick on the cobblestones, swaggering but hurrying, as if afraid to be caught at what he had done.

"I paid half a crown for the next issue of that magazine, and there it was in print! One of my sketches, 'A Dinner at Poplar Walk,' I think it was. I remember how it felt to see my words in print for the very first time."

Mary's voice took on a tone of chiding. "And you didn't even receive payment for the piece."

Dickens laughed. "What did it matter then? I was speaking to a whole world of readers! People were reading what I had written. I walked up and down Westminster Hall for half an hour. My eyes could hardly see, I was so excited!"

"Yet now you grow angry at anyone who prints even a bit of your correspondence without offering you royalties."

Dickens stiffened. "They make enormous amounts of money off me just by placing my name on their masthead! Pirates have made me lose thousands of pounds by flaunting the copyright law."

She had touched a sore spot, but he did not want to ruin their short time together by arguing. He softened his voice to change the subject. "These memories are delightful, Mary. Show me more!"

Her expression remained solemn. "Do not thank me until you have seen them all. Some of them may not be so precious, though they are as important."

Dickens felt a chill from inside. "What do you mean?" His tone spoke plainly that he did not want to hear the answer.

"Our time grows short," she said. "Quick! You must see one last memory of your past."

As she led him down the street, the sky darkened into night, growing blacker with each step they took. Greenish-white glows from gas street lights made the scene shift with a harsh mixture of glares and shadows. As Mary hurried him along, Dickens saw the buildings again, recognizing the brick facade, the wrought-iron fence, the decorative lintels and arches of Mecklenburgh Square.

As they approached, Dickens saw a tall man open the wrought-iron gate in front of a three-storey brick home. He was accompanied by two women, one larger and hanging on the man's arm, the other thin and delicate with dark hair pinned up under a bonnet. The man gestured for them both to precede him through the gate, then caught up with them under the rounded arch of the doorway. They all seemed to be laughing and enjoying themselves.

Dickens stood trembling, refusing to go another step. Mary pulled at him, but he closed his eyes. "No, Mary! Oh no, no!"

But she was insistent and drew him stumbling toward the door. "Was I not always a good friend to you, Charles? Without this visit, you cannot hope to receive everything I bring to you."

She led him through the half-open door into the rented

home where young Charles Dickens lived with his new wife Kate and her sixteen-year-old sister Mary.

"We had just gone to the theater, do you remember?" Mary said in a distant voice, as if she barely remembered herself. "It was late when we got home, about one o'clock in the morning. I had gone up to bed—"

"Stop!" he said. He had spent years with every detail of that evening pounding in his head, haunting his nightmares. There, in front of him, in the old house he and Kate and the children had left only a short time ago, he watched a younger, carefree version of himself removing his coat and handing it to the maid. He set his walking stick against the rail of the stairs, tossed his top hat behind him in a cocky gesture to hit the hat rack, but of course he missed and was just bending over to pick it up when he heard a choking cry from upstairs. Mary's voice.

It echoed in his ears, in his memory.

Sweating and shivering at the same time, Dickens watched himself, running up the steep staircase, grabbing the rail and launching himself upward with every step. "Mary!" his younger self cried in concerned surprise.

Watching the scene unfold again, the elder Dickens could not stop himself from shouting the same as he dashed up to the second-floor bedrooms. His footfalls made no sound on the steps.

Just inside the door of her room, Mary lay on the floor gasping, begging for help. Young Dickens sent for a doctor. His face was drawn and horrified. As he watched from his invisible vantage, the elder Dickens shook his head. "The doctor will not be able to do anything. They said you had a diseased heart, Mary. And now I have a broken one, all over again."

He turned to the spectral form of Mary, who watched without emotion the image of herself writhing on the floor. Young Dickens and Kate helped her onto the bed. She would die there the following day.

"This scene has haunted me more than any other," Dickens said. "Every letter I wrote for a year bore a black border in remembrance of you." He sighed, but it came out more like a moan. "When I was writing *The Old Curiosity Shop* and the time came when Little Nell had to die, I trembled for days beforehand, recalling your death. It cast the most horrible shadow upon me, and it was all I could do to keep moving at all."

Mary sighed, and he felt her spectral hand squeeze his. "Sometimes you are too sentimental, Charles."

Dickens saw that time had changed again. Mary Hogarth lay on her bed, but sunlight streamed through the windows, and the younger Charles Dickens held her in his arms, pulling the bedclothes over to keep her warm. He stroked her tangled hair … and felt her die in his arms.

Dickens watched himself take her cooling hand between his palms and slip one of the rings off her finger. "I will wear this ring of yours until the day I might join you," he said.

Dickens the observer stared at the ring on his own finger, still there after six years. To crush away the tears he rubbed his knuckles against his eyes. His head rang from the memory. Then the ringing sound became the chiming of the clock, and he and Mary's ghost returned to the warm sitting room in Devonshire Terrace. After all this time and all the years observed, the hour of midnight was just striking.

# STAVE THREE

DICKENS DREW A DEEP BREATH TO DRIVE BACK ALL the memories he had thought tucked away safe and sound. He warmed his hands over the fire in the sitting room, but his heart seemed to regulate its own warmth and chill. Exhausted, he shuffled back to his chair, but before he could turn round and sink into the cushions, before the clock finished striking the hour of twelve, Mary stopped him.

"We have no time to rest, Charles. This is a busy night for both of us."

He blinked at her, but now the delight of his reunion with Mary had been blunted by watching her death all over again. "I can't bear any more of my memories just now. I'm afraid of what else you might dredge from the mud of my past."

He squeezed his eyes shut and tried not to think of all the things he did not want to see again, all the black shadows of his younger life. But Mary's voice grew lighter.

"Not your past, Charles. Now we will go and see who you are right now. Until the clock strikes one, let us observe your present."

This baffled him, and he made sure to let her see it on his face. "What do you mean? I know who I am."

"Are you quite certain?"

"How can I not?"

In answer, Mary narrowed her eyes and looked at him with a penetrating gaze that made her seem centuries older than her sixteen-year-old form suggested.

"All right then, Spirit," he said submissively. "Conduct me where you will."

Mary went to the door of the sitting room and beckoned him. "Shall we go upstairs, then."

The hall was dim and orange, lit by candles Kate had left burning for him after she went to bed. The flickering light seemed to set off sparks from Mary's flowing white dress.

As they went up the stairs, Dickens felt light on his feet, and he wondered if he was really moving himself. When the fourth stair failed to creak under his step, he knew that this would be another shadow-show of visions, a theater performance Mary had staged for him.

She turned down the upstairs hall and opened the door to the wide Master Bedroom. By the sunlight in the window Dickens saw it was morning again, that very morning. Kate sat back in a rocking chair, working on another embroidered pillowcase; their maid Anne had drawn the pattern for it, as usual. Draped along the scrolled arm of the rocker hung limp bundles of bright threads. Kate shifted and tried to be comfortable, but her pregnancy made her look awkward no matter what she did. Her eyes, her cheeks, everything about her looked bloated, especially in contrast to the shining spirit of her sister. Kate's face looked like a poor reproduction of Mary's carved out of a potato.

Three of the four children sat in the room with her: little

Katey and Mamie peered at a book showing sketches of knights in shining armor; baby Walter lay on the bed making sounds like the water draining out of a wash basin.

"Kate sits here all day and does nothing," Dickens said. "Not at all like you, Mary. She takes no interest in my activities—"

Mary cut him off abruptly. "What would you have her do? The baby is due in less than a month. She watches the children, makes certain they refrain from bothering you, though many times they bother her to no end. Do you even notice?"

Interrupting her, the door burst open and five-year-old Charley ran in with tears brimming in his eyes. The boy made hiccupping noises and brushed past Dickens, missing him by no more than an inch, but he did not even see his father. In his small hand he held a little white note and a pincushion.

Kate looked up from her embroidery, saw the note, and allowed a brief and surprising expression of anger to flicker behind her eyes. Dickens remembered writing the note himself and placing it on Charley's bed, after he had completed his daily inspection of the household.

"What is it, Charley?" Kate asked. Her voice sounded soothing. Mamie and Katie turned the pages of their book, studiously ignoring their brother's anguish, while the baby kept gurgling.

The boy had to snuffle twice before he could hand her the note. His mother had no chance to read it before he burst out, "I only forgot to put my brown shoes in their box. I left 'em by my bed. I was going to." He drew a shaking breath and tried to fend off his tears long enough to speak what disturbed him the most. "And tomorrow's Christmas!"

Kate shook her head. "Don't expect mere Christmas to

make your father an easier man. What reason has he to be merry?" She smiled at the boy. "We'll have to make twice as merry ourselves!"

Dickens remained at the door, stung, as Kate heaved herself out of the rocking chair. She set her embroidery aside, fumbling but unable to catch a packet of bright green thread that unraveled and spilled onto the floor. She paid it no heed and gave the boy a gentle hug.

"Look at this, Charles," Mary's spirit said from across the room. She ran her translucent fingers over the frame of a small watercolor portrait showing the four children at play. "Do you remember it?"

Indeed he did—it was the going-away gift from a painter friend when he and Kate had departed for six months to see America. Dickens insisted on leaving the four children behind, claiming that the stress of travel and the inconvenience of having them along would be detrimental to his own activities.

Kate had mourned the thought of being separated from her children for half a year and begged not to go, but Dickens went ahead with the plans, the arrangements, the packing. Finally, Dickens sent his ebullient actor friend William Macready to speak to Kate and, as instructed, Macready gruffly told Mrs. Dickens that a wife's duty was to accompany her husband wherever he wished to go, and to be happy doing it. Kate took only the watercolor portrait of the children to keep her company; she propped it up in their room every night during the journey.

"You dragged my sister against her will to a foreign land she had no wish to see. The sea trip was the roughest passage for years. You never asked her if perhaps she would like to include something in your plans. But instead you took her to see you speak, to see you read aloud and give perfor-mances on the stage. You travelled to visit Washington Irving and Edgar Allan Poe and Henry Longfellow, and what did she profit from it all? The chance to hear you quietly insult your hosts and America in general, to complain about conditions there?"

Dickens took a step back out to the hall, and Mary's spirit whisked across the floor, passing through Katie and Mamie by their picture book. The anger in her eyes frightened him. This was not the type of visitation he had expected at all.

"Can we not see something else, Mary? I beg you!"

"Of course," she said, passing him and flowing back down the stairs. "Let's go watch the great Charles Dickens at work."

Still light on his feet, he dashed after her as Mary went down the hall to his writing study. Inside, he saw the new fire licking at fresh logs in the large fireplace. It was the first blaze of the morning, and he had added enough logs to keep it burning for a long time; he knew he was bound to be distracted by his writing and pay it no attention.

Dickens saw himself sitting at the desk, bent over a sheet of paper with pen in hand and inkwell nearby. A jumbled stack of papers lay at his left elbow, with one page nearly falling to the floor. A smudged thumbprint from a spilled drop of ink obscured a word in the margin. The only sounds in the room were the scratching of pen against paper, a rapid clink into the inkwell, the sizzling sound of the fire, and his own rapid breathing.

But as Dickens stood and watched the scene, he heard a rustle and saw little Mamie bundled in a blanket on the sofa. Her face had the rubbed-raw blush of one recovering from a fever. She propped a book on her bent knees. Keeping both eyes on her father at his desk, Mamie very carefully turned the page, as if terrified she might make a sound.

"I remember this day! A week ago—Mamie was sick, and I told her it would be all right if she wanted to rest in my study while I worked." He turned and looked to Mary for reassurance.

"You don't appear to be paying much attention to your daughter." Mary's voice remained cold.

The Dickens at the desk sprang to his feet and ran to a small mirror on the wall. He pushed his face to the reflection, opened his mouth, made bizarre contortions of his lips and eyebrows, then ran back to the desk. Picking up his pen, he scribbled down an entire paragraph without stopping, tilting the pen at an extreme angle to keep the words flowing without interrupting the sentence to dip into the ink again.

A moment later he stood up, went to the mirror once more, and proceeded to have a stop-and-start conversation with himself.

"It's nothing unusual," Dickens said to Mary. "Sometimes I get rather involved with my characters." But he felt his cheeks burning at this intrusion into a private moment as he worked. "It helps me stage some of my scenes."

But Mary seemed not at all concerned about that, looking instead at the girl on the sofa. Mamie watched her father's actions, bewildered and frightened, but she made not a sound.

"Your children are afraid of you, Charles. They see you as a whirlwind, always busy, never to be disturbed. You're a great mystery to them."

"Nonsense, they love me. I am their father!"

"You are a stranger."

Upset and impatient, Dickens stepped back out to the hall, turning his back on the scene in the study. "I presume you have some design with these pantomimes, Mary. Get on with it."

She took his hand, and this time it felt colder than ever. "Follow me, then. We'll take a walk outside." She threw open the front door to a sunny winter's afternoon, and they set foot on a street deep in the heart of London. The great house on Devonshire Terrace vanished behind them as they stepped into the bustle of activity. Dickens saw that they left no footprints in the snow.

They moved unhindered by the constant stream of passersby, the businessmen, the beggars. Coming from behind, Dickens recognized the man stumping along at a furious, distracted pace. He was dressed in a fur greatcoat over a brown frock coat, then a waistcoat in red from which a gold watch chain dangled. Two linked diamond pins fastened an extravagant cravat poking up around his Adam's apple. Mary hurried up beside the man, dragging her companion along.

"What are you trying to show me here, Mary? I know I like to walk, sometimes as much as thirty miles in a single day. It helps me to plan my stories, to converse with my characters. And I know very well what I look like."

"Do you know what you look like?" Mary asked, pulling him around to face the image of himself. The man kept walking ahead, eyes cast down, with steam from the cold air spurting out of his nose. "Look closely. See yourself not posing for the mirror."

Dickens inspected the familiar clean-shaven boyish-faced man, with wide nose and thick lips, long brown hair curling around his ears. But then he saw the shadows under the eyes, the sagging weariness in his defiant stride, the hunch of the shoulders, the tight frown heavy on his lips.

"I thought you said this would be visions of the present," Dickens said. "Surely this must be me some years in the future."

Mary shook her head. "No, that is how you appear to others even now. You appear harried, overworked, with never enough time. Constantly pushing yourself beyond goals no man could meet."

"With good reason!" he said, turning defensively toward her. "Is it so quiet in the grave that you can't hear them shouting how Charles Dickens has lost his popularity? The last installments of 'The Old Curiosity Shop' were selling a hundred thousand copies a week, but now 'Barnaby Rudge' barely sells a third of that, even at its best!"

His eyes blazed at her, and he stopped walking. Mary faced him, as the other image of Dickens continued his lonely walk along the streets, muttering to himself.

"I took a year away from writing to travel in America, and when I returned I thought the public would be hungry for my work, waiting to snap up anything I might do. But my *American Notes* received nothing but a cool reception from my readers. They used to snap up every tid-bit so eagerly—are they all tired of it now? This week's installment of 'Martin Chuzzlewit' is selling only twenty thousand copies, no matter what I do."

Mary's face grew stern, an alien expression on the girl he had cherished for so long in his dreams and nightmares. "And how much time do you waste giving speeches, attending gaudy social events? And that's only when you're not losing your temper with your friends or shouting at your publisher, or carrying on your endless fight for a reformed copyright law."

"The pirates are stealing me blind with bastard copies of my stories!"

"You don't seem to be doing much good work with the money you already possess. What good would you do with more of it?"

Dickens made no answer, but Mary had not finished taunting him. "You write weekly sketches, you work on two novels at a time, you write one-act farces and you star in them as well. No wonder your children don't know their father; no wonder dear Kate ignores you in simple defense against how you ignore her."

"But writing is my business!" Dickens said, crossing his arms over the gaps in his robe.

"Business!" cried Mary, "Mankind is your business. Don't you realize that a single story from you could do more good work than the House of Commons can manage in a year? In your constant challenge to produce more and more, you've forgotten what stories mean. Don't you remember your passion for a story that demands to be told? Or are you more interested in instant projects to increase your fame—if only for the moment?"

He stammered, "But, but that is not how I think of it at all."

Mary turned and pointed to the figure of Charles Dickens still striding away. "Look at him, walking as fast as he can but with his eyes to the ground. He'll reach his destination and go right past it without even knowing. You are a writer, Charles, surely you can appreciate such a metaphor?"

Dickens, feeling a heavy weight inside his chest, turned away. "I want to go back inside now."

Mary stopped in front of a leatherworker's shop and grasped the handle of the door. Behind the glass, Dickens could see only shadows of the proprietor and customers moving about. Before she opened the door, Mary softened her expression into gentle girlishness.

"Think of your children," she said, "and the story that Kate tells them of the three little pigs. Is it better to build a hundred huts of straw, or one or two fortresses of stone?"

She opened the door. "Stop writing books of straw."

He followed her inside, into his own sitting room again. The single chime rang out into the room as the clock struck one.

## STAVE FOUR

I HAVE ONLY ONE MORE THING TO SHOW YOU, Charles," Mary said to him. "A glimpse of things yet to come."

Dickens wanted to go nearer the fire, but found he could not move. "I think I fear that more than the other images." He realized his voice sounded thin.

"But I know you must have good intentions in your heart." Mary's eyes twinkled, and she flashed a smile at him. Once again she looked the playful sixteen-year-old, and his heart began to ache. "Stop your worrying. You may even enjoy this."

With a lilt in her step, Mary crossed the sitting room to a door Dickens had never seen before. It looked dark and narrow, perhaps a place where Captain Murderer would keep his blades for trimming wives into bite-sized pieces. Mary drew the door open without a creak. The firelight sparkled on the brasswork of the knob, which was different from any of the ornate latches Dickens had installed on the other mahogany doors.

Inside, he could see a shadowy passage, lit by white glow along the ceilings, as harsh as gaslight but not the same. Mary snatched his hand and drew him inside. He tried to resist, but his feet felt like leaden weights hooked to puppet strings.

The warm light of the sitting room hearth dwindled into nothing and vanished as they stepped forward. The air felt cool and smelled musty. The room was too dark to be observed with any accuracy, but Dickens glanced around, anxious to know what kind of room it was.

As his eyes adjusted he saw that the narrow walls were not walls at all, but shelves. Book shelves, filled with row upon row of bound volumes. "What is this place, Mary? A library perhaps?"

She stopped in front of a long shelf and raised her hand. Around them the light grew brighter, and he could distinguish all the books of different heights and sizes, with cloth or leather bindings of black, blue, brown. "Have a look at this one, Charles." With a crook of her finger, she tugged the first volume on the shelf a little way out. He squinted down at the gold-stamped letters on the spine.

"Why, that's my *Pickwick*! In an edition I have never seen." He made a small groan. "Someone else has pirated it, then!"

Mary's gentle laughter sounded like a bird in the forest. "Have you forgotten that we stepped into your future? Things yet to come."

Dickens ran his fingers over the spines. "And here's *Oliver Twist*, and *The Old Curiosity Shop!*" But as he continued down the line he stopped. "*Hard Times? A Tale of Two Cities? Great Expectations? Bleak House? The Mystery of Edwin Drood? David*

*Copperfield?*" He looked at her, dazed. "Who are all these people? Where are these places? Did I write so many books?"

Mary seemed entranced by the delight she saw on his face. "Of course." He reached out to pull one of the books from the shelves, but Mary stopped him. Sliding the volume back into place, she shook her head. "That is forbidden. If you'd like to learn these characters and know these stories, then you must write them yourself. Only that way can you, and the world, have these books."

He continued to stare at his own name engraved on the spines as if on a monument, CHARLES DICKENS. The thought of all those novels whirled in his imagination; he felt his fingers itching to get back to his pen and paper. Then he remembered the other things Mary had showed him that evening.

"Here is something you will enjoy even more," Mary said as she turned to the opposite shelf, and he saw more books, so many that they were stacked on top of each other, piled up out of sight, causing the shelves to bow in the middle. His name appeared on many of those spines, often in the titles. "Biographies of you, critical treatises, textbooks. The scholars have had as much enjoyment chronicling your life as studying your novels."

Dickens could only gape in astonishment. He felt his vision going dim with euphoria. He had never imagined this, not even in his most pretentious fantasies.

Mary took down one of the tomes and flipped to a page, then began to read in the flickering light. "'Charles Dickens was a great English novelist and one of the most popular writers of all time. A keen observer of life, Dickens had a great understanding of people. He showed sympathy for the poor and helpless, and mocked and criticized the selfish, the greedy, the cruel.'"

She closed the book with a slam and a smile. "What you will find even more remarkable, I think, is that the passage I just read will be written *more than a century after your death.* Your own fame will outshine that of Walter Scott, and Poe and Irving and Longfellow, all those you so admire."

Dickens had to grasp at one of the shelves to keep from falling backward. By the stiffness he felt on his face, he knew he must be grinning like an idiot. But then a suspicion of her own words cast a cloud across his thoughts. "Answer me one question, Mary—are these the images of things that *will* be, or are they the images of things that *may* be only?"

Mary began to walk back down the long corridor of shelves toward the sitting room.

"Mary! Tell me!" His slippers made skittering noises on the hard floor as he ran to catch up with her.

She stood at the door out into the firelit room. "Perhaps. But you must remember that your writing is not about *writing,* but about people. As is your life. It won't matter how clever you are, how many projects you can juggle at once, how many instances your name appears in the newspapers. You have a power to move the world if you choose to do so. But will you make the effort?"

Dickens pushed back into the sitting room. "Yes, I will! I won't forget the lessons you taught me."

He felt like dancing. The hands on the clock had somehow returned to midnight, and as he looked the hour began to chime once more.

Mary stood alone in the center of the room, and her white gown took on a grayish tinge, as if shadows seeped into the fabric. Her skin seemed paler than before, with a shimmering quality like cheap candlewax running into puddles.

"Now I must leave you, Charles. My time here is finished. Look to see me no more. And look that, for your own sake, you remember what has passed between us!" She stepped backward toward the window, fading as she went. Dickens reached for her, but the euphoria made him numb to the thought of never seeing her ghost again.

"Wait!" he called. "You've given me a gift beyond measure. Isn't there something I can do for you? Some way I can repay you?"

Mary continued to dissolve into the air, but at the last moment she turned her gaze full on him. "Write me a Christmas story," she said.

And when the last stroke of twelve had chimed, her ghost vanished completely.

Charles Dickens remained before the glowing hearth for a full hour, watching the logs slump into embers, before he finally turned and left the sitting room, going to the stairs that led to his bed. Kate would be long asleep, but he would do his best not to disturb her. As his foot fell on the fourth step, the creaking wood reminded him that he was whole and substantial, and alive. As were his family and his friends.

*A Christmas story?* he thought. His head pounded with the dizzying memories of the evening, and he knew sleep would be a long time coming.

He wondered if he would get any ideas.

# A CHRISTMAS CAROL

# CHARLES DICKENS

Mr. Fezziwig's Ball.

London Chapman & Hall 186 Strand.

# PREFACE

I have endeavoured in this Ghostly little book to raise the Ghost of an idea which shall not put my readers out of humour with themselves, with each other, with the season, or with me. May it haunt their house pleasantly, and no one wish to lay it.

Their faithful Friend and Servant,

—C. D.
—December, 1843

# CHARACTERS

Bob Cratchit, clerk to Ebenezer Scrooge.

Peter Cratchit, a son of the preceding.

Tim Cratchit ("Tiny Tim"), a cripple, youngest son of Bob
Cratchit.

Mr. Fezziwig, a kind-hearted, jovial old merchant.
Fred, Scrooge's nephew.

Ghost of Christmas Past, a phantom showing things past.

Ghost of Christmas Present, a spirit of a kind, generous, and
hearty nature.

Ghost of Christmas Yet to Come, an apparition showing the
shadows of things which yet may happen.

Ghost of Jacob Marley, a spectre of Scrooge's former partner in business.

Joe, a marine-store dealer and receiver of stolen goods.

Ebenezer Scrooge, a grasping, covetous old man, the surviving partner of the firm of Scrooge and Marley.

Mr. Topper, a bachelor.

Dick Wilkins, a fellow apprentice of Scrooge's.

Belle, a comely matron, an old sweetheart of Scrooge's.

Caroline, wife of one of Scrooge's debtors.

Mrs. Cratchit, wife of Bob Cratchit.

Belinda and Martha Cratchit, daughters of the preceding.

Mrs. Dilber, a laundress.

Fan, the sister of Scrooge.

Mrs. Fezziwig, the worthy partner of Mr. Fezziwig.

# STAVE ONE

## Marley's Ghost

MARLEY WAS DEAD, TO BEGIN WITH. THERE IS NO doubt whatever about that. The register of his burial was signed by the clergyman, the clerk, the undertaker, and the chief mourner. Scrooge signed it. And Scrooge's name was good upon 'Change for anything he chose to put his hand to. Old Marley was as dead as a door-nail.

Mind! I don't mean to say that I know of my own knowledge, what there is particularly dead about a door-nail. I might have been inclined, myself, to regard a coffin-nail as the deadest piece of ironmongery in the trade. But the wisdom of our ancestors is in the simile; and my unhallowed hands shall not disturb it, or the country's done for. You will, therefore, permit me to repeat, emphatically, that Marley was as dead as a door-nail.

Scrooge knew he was dead? Of course he did. How could

it be otherwise? Scrooge and he were partners for I don't know how many years. Scrooge was his sole executor, his sole administrator, his sole assign, his sole residuary legatee, his sole friend, and sole mourner. And even Scrooge was not so dreadfully cut up by the sad event but that he was an excellent man of business on the very day of the funeral, and solemnised it with an undoubted bargain.

The mention of Marley's funeral brings me back to the point I started from. There is no doubt that Marley was dead. This must be distinctly understood, or nothing wonderful can come of the story I am going to relate. If we were not perfectly convinced that Hamlet's father died before the play began, there would be nothing more remarkable in his taking a stroll at night, in an easterly wind, upon his own ramparts, than there would be in any other middle-aged gentleman rashly turning out after dark in a breezy spot—say St. Paul's Churchyard, for instance—literally to astonish his son's weak mind.

Scrooge never painted out Old Marley's name. There it stood, years afterwards, above the warehouse door: Scrooge and Marley. The firm was known as Scrooge and Marley. Sometimes people new to the business called Scrooge Scrooge, and sometimes Marley, but he answered to both names. It was all the same to him.

Oh! but he was a tight-fisted hand at the grindstone, Scrooge! a squeezing, wrenching, grasping, scraping, clutching, covetous old sinner! Hard and sharp as flint, from which no steel had ever struck out generous fire; secret, and self-contained, and solitary as an oyster. The cold within him froze his old features, nipped his pointed nose, shrivelled his cheek, stiffened his gait; made his eyes red, his thin lips blue; and spoke out shrewdly in his grating voice. A frosty rime was on his head, and on his eyebrows, and his wiry chin. He carried his own low temperature always about with him; he iced his office in the dog-days, and didn't thaw it one degree at Christmas.

External heat and cold had little influence on Scrooge. No warmth could warm, no wintry weather chill him. No wind that blew was bitterer than he, no falling snow was more intent upon its purpose, no pelting rain less open to entreaty. Foul weather didn't know where to have him. The heaviest rain, and snow, and hail, and sleet could boast of the advantage over him in only one respect. They often 'came down' handsomely, and Scrooge never did.

Nobody ever stopped him in the street to say, with gladsome looks, 'My dear Scrooge, how are you? When will you come to see me?' No beggars implored him to bestow a trifle, no children asked him what it was o'clock, no man or woman ever once in all his life inquired the way to such and such a place, of Scrooge. Even the blind men's dogs appeared to know him; and, when they saw him coming on, would tug their owners into doorways and up courts; and then would wag their tails as though they said, 'No eye at all is better than an evil eye, dark master!'

But what did Scrooge care? It was the very thing he liked. To edge his way along the crowded paths of life, warning all human sympathy to keep its distance, was what the knowing ones call 'nuts' to Scrooge.

Once upon a time—of all the good days in the year, on Christmas Eve—old Scrooge sat busy in his counting-house. It was cold, bleak, biting weather; foggy withal; and he could hear the people in the court outside go wheezing up and down, beating their hands upon their breasts, and stamping their feet upon the pavement stones to warm them. The City clocks had only just gone three, but it was quite dark already —it had not been light all day—and candles were flaring in the windows of the neighbouring offices, like ruddy smears upon the palpable brown air. The fog came pouring in at every chink and keyhole, and was so dense without, that, although the court was of the narrowest, the houses opposite were mere phantoms. To see the dingy cloud come drooping down, obscuring everything, one might have thought that nature lived hard by, and was brewing on a large scale.

The door of Scrooge's counting-house was open, that he might keep his eye upon his clerk, who in a dismal little cell beyond, a sort of tank, was copying letters. Scrooge had a very small fire, but the clerk's fire was so very much smaller that it looked like one coal. But he couldn't replenish it, for Scrooge kept the coal-box in his own room; and so surely as the clerk came in with the shovel, the master predicted that it would be necessary for them to part. Wherefore the clerk put on his white comforter, and tried to warm himself at the candle; in which effort, not being a man of strong imagination, he failed.

'A merry Christmas, uncle! God save you!' cried a cheerful voice. It was the voice of Scrooge's nephew, who came upon him so quickly that this was the first intimation he had of his approach.

'Bah!' said Scrooge. 'Humbug!'

He had so heated himself with rapid walking in the fog and frost, this nephew of Scrooge's, that he was all in a glow; his face was ruddy and handsome; his eyes sparkled, and his breath smoked again.

'Christmas a humbug, uncle!' said Scrooge's nephew. 'You don't mean that, I am sure?'

'I do,' said Scrooge. 'Merry Christmas! What right have

you to be merry? What reason have you to be merry? You're poor enough.'

'Come, then,' returned the nephew gaily. 'What right have you to be dismal? What reason have you to be morose? You're rich enough.'

Scrooge, having no better answer ready on the spur of the moment, said, 'Bah!' again; and followed it up with 'Humbug!'

'Don't be cross, uncle!' said the nephew.

'What else can I be,' returned the uncle, 'when I live in such a world of fools as this? Merry Christmas! Out upon merry Christmas! What's Christmas-time to you but a time for paying bills without money; a time for finding yourself a year older, and not an hour richer; a time for balancing your books, and having every item in 'em through a round dozen of months presented dead against you? If I could work my will,' said Scrooge indignantly, 'every idiot who goes about with "Merry Christmas" on his lips should be boiled with his own pudding, and buried with a stake of holly through his heart. He should!'

'Uncle!' pleaded the nephew.

'Nephew!' returned the uncle sternly, 'keep Christmas in your own way, and let me keep it in mine.'

'Keep it!' repeated Scrooge's nephew. 'But you don't keep it.'

'Let me leave it alone, then,' said Scrooge. 'Much good may it do you! Much good it has ever done you!'

'There are many things from which I might have derived good, by which I have not profited, I dare say,' returned the nephew; 'Christmas among the rest. But I am sure I have always thought of Christmas-time, when it has come round —apart from the veneration due to its sacred name and origin, if anything belonging to it can be apart from that—as a good time; a kind, forgiving, charitable, pleasant time; the only time I know of, in the long calendar of the year, when men and women seem by one consent to open their shut-up hearts freely, and to think of people below them as if they really were fellow-passengers to the grave, and not another race of creatures bound on other journeys. And therefore, uncle, though it has never put a scrap of gold or silver in my pocket, I believe that it *has* done me good and *will* do me good; and I say, God bless it!'

The clerk in the tank involuntarily applauded. Becoming immediately sensible of the impropriety, he poked the fire, and extinguished the last frail spark for ever.

'Let me hear another sound from *you*,' said Scrooge, 'and you'll keep your Christmas by losing your situation! You're quite a powerful speaker, sir,' he added, turning to his nephew. 'I wonder you don't go into Parliament.'

'Don't be angry, uncle. Come! Dine with us to-morrow.'

Scrooge said that he would see him—Yes, indeed he did. He went the whole length of the expression, and said that he would see him in that extremity first.

'But why?' cried Scrooge's nephew. 'Why?'

'Why did you get married?' said Scrooge.

'Because I fell in love.'

'Because you fell in love!' growled Scrooge, as if that were the only one thing in the world more ridiculous than a merry Christmas. 'Good afternoon!'

'Nay, uncle, but you never came to see me before that happened. Why give it as a reason for not coming now?'

'Good afternoon,' said Scrooge.

'I want nothing from you; I ask nothing of you; why cannot we be friends?'

'Good afternoon!' said Scrooge.

'I am sorry, with all my heart, to find you so resolute. We have never had any quarrel to which I have been a party. But I have made the trial in homage to Christmas, and I'll keep my Christmas humour to the last. So A Merry Christmas, uncle!'

'Good afternoon,' said Scrooge.

'And A Happy New Year!'

'Good afternoon!' said Scrooge.

His nephew left the room without an angry word, notwithstanding. He stopped at the outer door to bestow the greetings of the season on the clerk, who, cold as he was, was warmer than Scrooge; for he returned them cordially.

'There's another fellow,' muttered Scrooge, who over-heard him: 'my clerk, with fifteen shillings a week, and a wife and family, talking about a merry Christmas. I'll retire to Bedlam.'

This lunatic, in letting Scrooge's nephew out, had let two other people in. They were portly gentlemen, pleasant to behold, and now stood, with their hats off, in Scrooge's office. They had books and papers in their hands, and bowed to him.

'Scrooge and Marley's, I believe,' said one of the gentlemen, referring to his list. 'Have I the pleasure of addressing Mr. Scrooge, or Mr. Marley?'

'Mr. Marley has been dead these seven years,' Scrooge replied. 'He died seven years ago, this very night.'

'We have no doubt his liberality is well represented by his surviving partner,' said the gentleman, presenting his credentials.

It certainly was; for they had been two kindred spirits. At the ominous word 'liberality' Scrooge frowned, and shook his head, and handed the credentials back.

'At this festive season of the year, Mr. Scrooge,' said the gentleman, taking up a pen, 'it is more than usually desirable that we should make some slight provision for the poor and destitute, who suffer greatly at the present time. Many thousands are in want of common necessaries; hundreds of thousands are in want of common comforts, sir.'

'Are there no prisons?' asked Scrooge.

'Plenty of prisons,' said the gentleman, laying down the pen again.

'And the Union workhouses?' demanded Scrooge. 'Are they still in operation?'

'They are. Still,' returned the gentleman, 'I wish I could say they were not.'

'The Treadmill and the Poor Law are in full vigour, then?' said Scrooge.

'Both very busy, sir.'

'Oh! I was afraid, from what you said at first, that something had occurred to stop them in their useful course,' said Scrooge. 'I am very glad to hear it.'

'Under the impression that they scarcely furnish Christian cheer of mind or body to the multitude,' returned the gentleman, 'a few of us are endeavouring to raise a fund to buy the Poor some meat and drink, and means of warmth. We choose this time, because it is a time, of all others, when Want is keenly felt, and Abundance rejoices. What shall I put you down for?'

'Nothing!' Scrooge replied.

'You wish to be anonymous?'

'I wish to be left alone,' said Scrooge. 'Since you ask me what I wish, gentlemen, that is my answer. I don't make merry myself at Christmas, and I can't afford to make idle people merry. I help to support the establishments I have mentioned—they cost enough: and those who are badly off must go there.'

'Many can't go there; and many would rather die.'

'If they would rather die,' said Scrooge, 'they had better do it, and decrease the surplus population. Besides—excuse me—I don't know that.'

'But you might know it,' observed the gentleman.

'It's not my business,' Scrooge returned. 'It's enough for a man to understand his own business, and not to interfere with other people's. Mine occupies me constantly. Good afternoon, gentlemen!'

Seeing clearly that it would be useless to pursue their point, the gentlemen withdrew. Scrooge resumed his labours with an improved opinion of himself, and in a more facetious temper than was usual with him.

Meanwhile the fog and darkness thickened so, that people ran about with flaring links, proffering their services to go before horses in carriages, and conduct them on their way. The ancient tower of a church, whose gruff old bell was always peeping slyly down at Scrooge out of a Gothic window in the wall, became invisible, and struck the hours and quarters in the clouds, with tremulous vibrations afterwards, as if its teeth were chattering in its frozen head up there. The cold became intense. In the main street, at the corner of the court, some labourers were repairing the gas-pipes, and had lighted a great fire in a brazier, round which a party of ragged men and boys were gathered: warming their hands and winking their eyes before the blaze in rapture. The water-plug being left in solitude, its overflowings suddenly congealed, and turned to misanthropic ice. The brightness of the shops, where holly sprigs and berries crackled in the lamp heat of the windows, made pale faces ruddy as they passed. Poulterers' and grocers' trades became a splendid joke: a glorious pageant, with which it was next to impossible to believe that such dull principles as bargain and sale had anything to do. The Lord Mayor, in the stronghold of the mighty Mansion House, gave orders to his fifty cooks and butlers to keep Christmas as a Lord Mayor's household should; and even the little tailor, whom he had fined five shillings on the previous Monday for being drunk and bloodthirsty in the streets, stirred up to-morrow's pudding in his garret, while his lean wife and the baby sallied out to buy the beef.

Foggier yet, and colder! Piercing, searching, biting cold. If the good St. Dunstan had but nipped the Evil Spirit's nose with a touch of such weather as that, instead of using his familiar weapons, then indeed he would have roared to lusty purpose. The owner of one scant young nose, gnawed and mumbled by the hungry cold as bones are gnawed by dogs, stooped down at Scrooge's keyhole to regale him with a Christmas carol; but, at the first sound of

> *'God bless you, merry gentleman,*
> *May nothing you dismay!'*

Scrooge seized the ruler with such energy of action that the singer fled in terror, leaving the keyhole to the fog, and even more congenial frost.

At length the hour of shutting up the counting-house arrived. With an ill-will Scrooge dismounted from his stool, and tacitly admitted the fact to the expectant clerk in the tank, who instantly snuffed his candle out, and put on his hat.

'You'll want all day to-morrow, I suppose?' said Scrooge.

'If quite convenient, sir.'

'It's not convenient,' said Scrooge, 'and it's not fair. If I was to stop half-a-crown for it, you'd think yourself ill used, I'll be bound?'

The clerk smiled faintly.

'And yet,' said Scrooge, 'you don't think *me* ill used when I pay a day's wages for no work.'

The clerk observed that it was only once a year.

'A poor excuse for picking a man's pocket every twenty-fifth of December!' said Scrooge, buttoning his greatcoat to the chin. 'But I suppose you must have the whole day. Be here all the earlier next morning.'

The clerk promised that he would; and Scrooge walked out with a growl. The office was closed in a twinkling, and the clerk, with the long ends of his white comforter dangling below his waist (for he boasted no greatcoat), went down a slide on Cornhill, at the end of a lane of boys, twenty times, in honour of its being Christmas Eve, and then ran home to Camden Town as hard as he could pelt, to play at blind man's-buff.

Scrooge took his melancholy dinner in his usual melancholy tavern; and having read all the newspapers, and beguiled the rest of the evening with his banker's book, went home to bed. He lived in chambers which had once belonged to his deceased partner. They were a gloomy suite of rooms, in a lowering pile of building up a yard, where it had so little business to be, that one could scarcely help fancying it must have run there when it was a young house, playing at hide-and-seek with other houses, and have forgotten the way out again. It was old enough now, and dreary enough; for nobody lived in it but Scrooge, the other rooms being all let out as offices. The yard was so dark that even Scrooge, who knew its every stone, was fain to grope with his hands. The fog and frost so hung about the black old gateway of the house, that it seemed as if the Genius of the Weather sat in mournful meditation on the threshold.

Now, it is a fact that there was nothing at all particular about the knocker on the door, except that it was very large. It is also a fact that Scrooge had seen it, night and morning, during his whole residence in that place; also that Scrooge had as little of what is called fancy about him as any man in the City of London, even including—which is a bold word— the corporation, aldermen, and livery. Let it also be borne in mind that Scrooge had not bestowed one thought on Marley since his last mention of his seven-years'-dead partner that afternoon. And then let any man explain to me, if he can, how it happened that Scrooge, having his key in the lock of the door, saw in the knocker, without its undergoing any intermediate process of change—not a knocker, but Marley's face.

Marley's face. It was not in impenetrable shadow, as the other objects in the yard were, but had a dismal light about it, like a bad lobster in a dark cellar. It was not angry or fero- cious, but looked at Scrooge as Marley used to look; with ghostly spectacles turned up on its ghostly forehead. The hair was curiously stirred, as if by breath or hot air; and, though the eyes were wide open, they were perfectly motionless. That, and its livid colour, made it horrible; but its horror seemed to be in spite of the face, and beyond its control, rather than a part of its own expression.

As Scrooge looked fixedly at this phenomenon, it was a knocker again.

To say that he was not startled, or that his blood was not conscious of a terrible sensation to which it had been a stranger from infancy, would be untrue. But he put his hand upon the key he had relinquished, turned it sturdily, walked in, and lighted his candle.

He *did* pause, with a moment's irresolution, before he shut the door; and he *did* look cautiously behind it first, as if he half expected to be terrified with the sight of Marley's pigtail sticking out into the hall. But there was nothing on the back of the door, except the screws and nuts that held the knocker on, so he said, 'Pooh, pooh!' and closed it with a bang.

The sound resounded through the house like thunder. Every room above, and every cask in the wine-merchant's cellars below, appeared to have a separate peal of echoes of its own. Scrooge was not a man to be frightened by echoes. He fastened the door, and walked across the hall, and up the stairs: slowly, too: trimming his candle as he went.

You may talk vaguely about driving a coach and six up a good old flight of stairs, or through a bad young Act of Parliament; but I mean to say you might have got a hearse up that staircase, and taken it broadwise, with the splinter-bar towards the wall, and the door towards the balustrades: and done it easy. There was plenty of width for that, and room to spare; which is perhaps the reason why Scrooge thought he saw a locomotive hearse going on before him in the gloom. Half-a-dozen gas-lamps out of the street wouldn't have lighted the entry too well, so you may suppose that it was pretty dark with Scrooge's dip.

Up Scrooge went, not caring a button for that. Darkness is cheap, and Scrooge liked it. But, before he shut his heavy door, he walked through his rooms to see that all was right. He had just enough recollection of the face to desire to do that.

Sitting-room, bedroom, lumber-room. All as they should

be. Nobody under the table, nobody under the sofa; a small fire in the grate; spoon and basin ready; and the little saucepan of gruel (Scrooge had a cold in his head) upon the hob. Nobody under the bed; nobody in the closet; nobody in his dressing-gown, which was hanging up in a suspicious attitude against the wall. Lumber-room as usual. Old fire-guard, old shoes, two fish baskets, washing-stand on three legs, and a poker.

Quite satisfied, he closed his door, and locked himself in; double locked himself in, which was not his custom. Thus secured against surprise, he took off his cravat; put on his dressing-gown and slippers, and his nightcap; and sat down before the fire to take his gruel.

It was a very low fire indeed; nothing on such a bitter night. He was obliged to sit close to it, and brood over it, before he could extract the least sensation of warmth from such a handful of fuel. The fireplace was an old one, built by some Dutch merchant long ago, and paved all round with quaint Dutch tiles, designed to illustrate the Scriptures. There were Cains and Abels, Pharaoh's daughters, Queens of Sheba, Angelic messengers descending through the air on clouds like feather-beds, Abrahams, Belshazzars, Apostles putting off to sea in butter-boats, hundreds of figures to attract his thoughts; and yet that face of Marley, seven years dead, came like the ancient Prophet's rod, and swallowed up the whole. If each smooth tile had been a blank at first, with power to shape some picture on its surface from the disjointed fragments of his thoughts, there would have been a copy of old Marley's head on every one.

'Humbug!' said Scrooge; and walked across the room.

After several turns he sat down again. As he threw his head back in the chair, his glance happened to rest upon a bell, a disused bell, that hung in the room, and communicated, for some purpose now forgotten, with a chamber in the highest storey of the building. It was with great astonishment, and with a strange, inexplicable dread, that, as he looked, he saw this bell begin to swing. It swung so softly in the outset that it scarcely made a sound; but soon it rang out loudly, and so did every bell in the house.

This might have lasted half a minute, or a minute, but it seemed an hour. The bells ceased, as they had begun, together. They were succeeded by a clanking noise deep down below as if some person were dragging a heavy chain over the casks in the wine-merchant's cellar. Scrooge then remembered to have heard that ghosts in haunted houses were described as dragging chains.

The cellar door flew open with a booming sound, and then he heard the noise much louder on the floors below; then coming up the stairs; then coming straight towards his door.

'It's humbug still!' said Scrooge. 'I won't believe it.'

His colour changed, though, when, without a pause, it came on through the heavy door and passed into the room before his eyes. Upon its coming in, the dying flame leaped up, as though it cried, 'I know him! Marley's Ghost!' and fell again.

Marley's Ghost.

London Chapman & Hall 186 Strand

The same face: the very same. Marley in his pigtail, usual waistcoat, tights, and boots; the tassels on the latter bristling, like his pigtail, and his coat-skirts, and the hair upon his head. The chain he drew was clasped about his middle. It was long, and wound about him like a tail; and it was made (for Scrooge observed it closely) of cash-boxes, keys, padlocks, ledgers, deeds, and heavy purses wrought in steel. His body was transparent: so that Scrooge, observing him, and looking through his waistcoat, could see the two buttons on his coat behind.

Scrooge had often heard it said that Marley had no bowels, but he had never believed it until now.

No, nor did he believe it even now. Though he looked the phantom through and through, and saw it standing before him; though he felt the chilling influence of its death-cold eyes, and marked the very texture of the folded kerchief bound about its head and chin, which wrapper he had not observed before, he was still incredulous, and fought against his senses.

'How now!' said Scrooge, caustic and cold as ever. 'What do you want with me?'

'Much!'—Marley's voice; no doubt about it.

'Who are you?'

'Ask me who I *was*.'

'Who *were* you, then?' said Scrooge, raising his voice. 'You're particular, for a shade.' He was going to say '*to* a shade,' but substituted this, as more appropriate.

'In life I was your partner, Jacob Marley.'

'Can you—can you sit down?' asked Scrooge, looking doubtfully at him.

'I can.'

'Do it, then.'

Scrooge asked the question, because he didn't know whether a ghost so transparent might find himself in a condition to take a chair; and felt that in the event of its being impossible, it might involve the necessity of an embarrassing explanation. But the Ghost sat down on the opposite side of the fireplace, as if he were quite used to it.

'You don't believe in me,' observed the Ghost.

'I don't,' said Scrooge.

'What evidence would you have of my reality beyond that of your own senses?'

'I don't know,' said Scrooge.

'Why do you doubt your senses?'

'Because,' said Scrooge, 'a little thing affects them. A slight disorder of the stomach makes them cheats. You may be an undigested bit of beef, a blot of mustard, a crumb of cheese, a fragment of an underdone potato. There's more of gravy than of grave about you, whatever you are!'

Scrooge was not much in the habit of cracking jokes, nor did he feel in his heart by any means waggish then. The truth is, that he tried to be smart, as a means of distracting his own attention, and keeping down his terror; for the spectre's voice disturbed the very marrow in his bones.

To sit staring at those fixed, glazed eyes in silence, for a moment, would play, Scrooge felt, the very deuce with him. There was something very awful, too, in the spectre's being provided with an infernal atmosphere of his own. Scrooge could not feel it himself, but this was clearly the case; for though the Ghost sat perfectly motionless, its hair, and skirts, and tassels were still agitated as by the hot vapour from an oven.

'You see this toothpick?' said Scrooge, returning quickly to the charge, for the reason just assigned; and wishing, though it were only for a second, to divert the vision's stony gaze from himself.

'I do,' replied the Ghost.

'You are not looking at it,' said Scrooge.

'But I see it,' said the Ghost, 'notwithstanding.'

'Well!' returned Scrooge, 'I have but to swallow this, and be for the rest of my days persecuted by a legion of goblins, all of my own creation. Humbug, I tell you: humbug!'

At this the spirit raised a frightful cry, and shook its chain with such a dismal and appalling noise, that Scrooge held on tight to his chair, to save himself from falling in a swoon. But how much greater was his horror when the phantom, taking off the bandage round his head, as if it were too warm to wear indoors, its lower jaw dropped down upon its breast!

Scrooge fell upon his knees, and clasped his hands before his face.

'Mercy!' he said. 'Dreadful apparition, why do you trouble me?'

'Man of the worldly mind!' replied the Ghost, 'do you believe in me or not?'

'I do,' said Scrooge; 'I must. But why do spirits walk the earth, and why do they come to me?'

'It is required of every man,' the Ghost returned, 'that the spirit within him should walk abroad among his fellow-men, and travel far and wide; and, if that spirit goes not forth in life, it is condemned to do so after death. It is doomed to wander through the world—oh, woe is me!—and witness what it cannot share, but might have shared on earth, and turned to happiness!'

Again the spectre raised a cry, and shook its chain and wrung its shadowy hands.

'You are fettered,' said Scrooge, trembling. 'Tell me why?'

'I wear the chain I forged in life,' replied the Ghost. 'I made it link by link, and yard by yard; I girded it on of my own free will, and of my own free will I wore it. Is its pattern strange to *you*?'

Scrooge trembled more and more.

'Or would you know,' pursued the Ghost, 'the weight and length of the strong coil you bear yourself? It was full as heavy and as long as this seven Christmas Eves ago. You have laboured on it since. It is a ponderous chain!'

Scrooge glanced about him on the floor, in the expectation of finding himself surrounded by some fifty or sixty fathoms of iron cable; but he could see nothing.

'Jacob!' he said imploringly. 'Old Jacob Marley, tell me more! Speak comfort to me, Jacob!'

'I have none to give,' the Ghost replied. 'It comes from other regions, Ebenezer Scrooge, and is conveyed by other ministers, to other kinds of men. Nor can I tell you what I would. A very little more is all permitted to me. I cannot rest, I cannot stay, I cannot linger anywhere. My spirit never walked beyond our counting-house—mark me;—in life my spirit never roved beyond the narrow limits of our money-changing hole; and weary journeys lie before me!'

It was a habit with Scrooge, whenever he became thoughtful, to put his hands in his breeches pockets. Pondering on what the Ghost had said, he did so now, but without lifting up his eyes, or getting off his knees.

'You must have been very slow about it, Jacob,' Scrooge observed in a business-like manner, though with humility and deference.

'Slow!' the Ghost repeated.

'Seven years dead,' mused Scrooge. 'And travelling all the time?'

'The whole time,' said the Ghost. 'No rest, no peace. Incessant torture of remorse.'

'You travel fast?' said Scrooge.

'On the wings of the wind,' replied the Ghost.

'You might have got over a great quantity of ground in seven years,' said Scrooge.

The Ghost, on hearing this, set up another cry, and clanked its chain so hideously in the dead silence of the night, that the Ward would have been justified in indicting it for a nuisance.

'Oh! captive, bound, and double-ironed,' cried the phantom, 'not to know that ages of incessant labour, by immortal creatures, for this earth must pass into eternity before the good of which it is susceptible is all developed! Not to know that any Christian spirit working kindly in its little sphere, whatever it may be, will find its mortal life too short for its vast means of usefulness! Not to know that no space of regret can make amends for one life's opportunities misused! Yet such was I! Oh, such was I!'

'But you were always a good man of business, Jacob,' faltered Scrooge, who now began to apply this to himself.

'Business!' cried the Ghost, wringing its hands again. 'Mankind was my business. The common welfare was my business; charity, mercy, forbearance, and benevolence were, all, my business. The dealings of my trade were but a drop of water in the comprehensive ocean of my business!'

It held up its chain at arm's-length, as if that were the cause of all its unavailing grief, and flung it heavily upon the ground again.

'At this time of the rolling year,' the spectre said, 'I suffer most. Why did I walk through crowds of fellow-beings with my eyes turned down, and never raise them to that blessed Star which led the Wise Men to a poor abode? Were there no poor homes to which its light would have conducted *me*?'

Scrooge was very much dismayed to hear the spectre going on at this rate, and began to quake exceedingly.

'Hear me!' cried the Ghost. 'My time is nearly gone.'

'I will,' said Scrooge. 'But don't be hard upon me! Don't be flowery, Jacob! Pray!'

'How it is that I appear before you in a shape that you can see, I may not tell. I have sat invisible beside you many and many a day.'

It was not an agreeable idea. Scrooge shivered, and wiped the perspiration from his brow.

'That is no light part of my penance,' pursued the Ghost. 'I am here to-night to warn you that you have yet a chance and hope of escaping my fate. A chance and hope of my procuring, Ebenezer.'

'You were always a good friend to me,' said Scrooge. 'Thankee!'

'You will be haunted,' resumed the Ghost, 'by Three Spirits.'

Scrooge's countenance fell almost as low as the Ghost's had done.

'Is that the chance and hope you mentioned, Jacob?' he demanded in a faltering voice.

'It is.'

'I—I think I'd rather not,' said Scrooge.

'Without their visits,' said the Ghost, 'you cannot hope to shun the path I tread. Expect the first to-morrow when the bell tolls One.'

'Couldn't I take 'em all at once, and have it over, Jacob?' hinted Scrooge.

'Expect the second on the next night at the same hour. The third, upon the next night when the last stroke of Twelve has ceased to vibrate. Look to see me no more; and look that, for your own sake, you remember what has passed between us!'

When it had said these words, the spectre took its wrapper from the table, and bound it round its head as before. Scrooge knew this by the smart sound its teeth made when the jaws were brought together by the bandage. He ventured to raise his eyes again, and found his supernatural visitor confronting him in an erect attitude, with its chain wound over and about its arm.

The apparition walked backward from him; and, at every step it took, the window raised itself a little, so that, when the spectre reached it, it was wide open. It beckoned Scrooge to approach, which he did. When they were within two paces of each other, Marley's Ghost held up its hand, warning him to come no nearer. Scrooge stopped.

Not so much in obedience as in surprise and fear; for, on the raising of the hand, he became sensible of confused noises in the air; incoherent sounds of lamentation and regret; wailings inexpressibly sorrowful and self-accusatory. The spectre, after listening for a moment, joined in the mournful dirge; and floated out upon the bleak, dark night.

Scrooge followed to the window: desperate in his curiosity. He looked out.

The air was filled with phantoms, wandering hither and thither in restless haste, and moaning as they went. Every one of them wore chains like Marley's Ghost; some few (they might be guilty governments) were linked together; none were free. Many had been personally known to Scrooge in their lives. He had been quite familiar with one old ghost in a white waistcoat, with a monstrous iron safe attached to its ankle, who cried piteously at being unable to assist a wretched woman with an infant, whom it saw below upon a doorstep. The misery with them all was clearly, that they sought to interfere, for good, in human matters, and had lost the power for ever.

Whether these creatures faded into mist, or mist

enshrouded them, he could not tell. But they and their spirit voices faded together; and the night became as it had been when he walked home.

Scrooge closed the window, and examined the door by which the Ghost had entered. It was double locked, as he had locked it with his own hands, and the bolts were undisturbed. He tried to say 'Humbug!' but stopped at the first syllable. And being, from the emotions he had undergone, or the fatigues of the day, or his glimpse of the Invisible World, or the dull conversation of the Ghost, or the lateness of the hour, much in need of repose, went straight to bed without undressing, and fell asleep upon the instant.

STAVE TWO




**The First of the Three Spirits**


WHEN SCROOGE AWOKE IT WAS SO DARK, THAT,
looking out of bed, he could scarcely distinguish the
transparent window from the opaque walls of his chamber. He was endeavouring to pierce the darkness with
his ferret eyes, when the chimes of a neighbouring
church struck the four quarters. So he listened for the
hour.

To his great astonishment, the heavy bell went on from
six to seven, and from seven to eight, and regularly up to
twelve; then stopped. Twelve! It was past two when he went
to bed. The clock was wrong. An icicle must have got into
the works. Twelve!

He touched the spring of his repeater, to correct this most
preposterous clock. Its rapid little pulse beat twelve, and
stopped.

'Why, it isn't possible,' said Scrooge, 'that I can have slept
through a whole day and far into another night. It isn't

possible that anything has happened to the sun, and this is twelve at noon!'

The idea being an alarming one, he scrambled out of bed, and groped his way to the window. He was obliged to rub the frost off with the sleeve of his dressing-gown before he could see anything; and could see very little then. All he could make out was, that it was still very foggy and extremely cold, and that there was no noise of people running to and fro, and making a great stir, as there unquestionably would have been if night had beaten off bright day, and taken possession of the world. This was a great relief, because 'Three days after sight of this First of Exchange pay to Mr. Ebenezer Scrooge or his order,' and so forth, would have become a mere United States security if there were no days to count by.

Scrooge went to bed again, and thought, and thought, and thought it over and over, and could make nothing of it. The more he thought, the more perplexed he was; and, the more he endeavoured not to think, the more he thought.

Marley's Ghost bothered him exceedingly. Every time he resolved within himself, after mature inquiry that it was all a dream, his mind flew back again, like a strong spring released, to its first position, and presented the same problem to be worked all through, 'Was it a dream or not?'

Scrooge lay in this state until the chime had gone three-quarters more, when he remembered, on a sudden, that the Ghost had warned him of a visitation when the bell tolled one. He resolved to lie awake until the hour was passed; and, considering that he could no more go to sleep than go to heaven, this was, perhaps, the wisest resolution in his power.

The quarter was so long, that he was more than once convinced he must have sunk into a doze unconsciously, and missed the clock. At length it broke upon his listening ear.

'Ding, dong!'

'A quarter past,' said Scrooge, counting.

'Ding, dong!'

'Half past,' said Scrooge.

'Ding, dong!'

'A quarter to it.' said Scrooge.

'Ding, dong!'

'The hour itself,' said Scrooge triumphantly, 'and nothing else!'

He spoke before the hour bell sounded, which it now did with a deep, dull, hollow, melancholy ONE. Light flashed up in the room upon the instant, and the curtains of his bed were drawn.

The curtains of his bed were drawn aside, I tell you, by a hand. Not the curtains at his feet, nor the curtains at his back, but those to which his face was addressed. The curtains of his bed were drawn aside; and Scrooge, starting up into a half-recumbent attitude, found himself face to face with the unearthly visitor who drew them: as close to it as I am now to you, and I am standing in the spirit at your elbow.

It was a strange figure—like a child; yet not so like a child as like an old man, viewed through some supernatural medium, which gave him the appearance of having receded from the view, and being diminished to a child's proportions. Its hair, which hung about its neck and down its back, was white, as if with age; and yet the face had not a wrinkle in it, and the tenderest bloom was on the skin. The arms were very long and muscular; the hands the same, as if its hold were of uncommon strength. Its legs and feet, most delicately formed, were, like those upper members, bare. It wore a tunic of the purest white; and round its waist was bound a lustrous belt, the sheen of which was beautiful. It held a branch of fresh green holly in its hand; and, in singular contradiction of that wintry emblem, had its dress trimmed with summer flowers. But the strangest thing about it was, that from the crown of its head there sprang a bright clear jet of light, by which all this was visible; and which was doubtless the occasion of its using, in its duller moments, a great extinguisher for a cap, which it now held under its arm.

Even this, though, when Scrooge looked at it with increasing steadiness, was *not* its strangest quality. For, as its belt sparkled and glittered, now in one part and now in another, and what was light one instant at another time was dark, so the figure itself fluctuated in its distinctness; being now a thing with one arm, now with one leg, now with twenty legs, now a pair of legs without a head, now a head without a body: of which dissolving parts no outline would be visible in the dense gloom wherein they melted away. And, in the very wonder of this, it would be itself again; distinct and clear as ever.

'Are you the Spirit, sir, whose coming was foretold to me?' asked Scrooge.

'I am!'

The voice was soft and gentle. Singularly low, as if, instead of being so close behind him, it were at a distance.

'Who and what are you?' Scrooge demanded.

'I am the Ghost of Christmas Past.'

'Long Past?' inquired Scrooge, observant of its dwarfish stature.

'No. Your past.'

Perhaps Scrooge could not have told anybody why, if anybody could have asked him; but he had a special desire to see the Spirit in his cap, and begged him to be covered.

'What!' exclaimed the Ghost, 'would you so soon put out,

with worldly hands, the light I give? Is it not enough that you are one of those whose passions made this cap, and force me through whole trains of years to wear it low upon my brow?'

Scrooge reverently disclaimed all intention to offend or any knowledge of having wilfully 'bonneted' the Spirit at any period of his life. He then made bold to inquire what business brought him there.

'Your welfare!' said the Ghost.

Scrooge expressed himself much obliged, but could not help thinking that a night of unbroken rest would have been more conducive to that end. The Spirit must have heard him thinking, for it said immediately—

'Your reclamation, then. Take heed!'

It put out its strong hand as it spoke, and clasped him gently by the arm.

'Rise! and walk with me!'

It would have been in vain for Scrooge to plead that the weather and the hour were not adapted to pedestrian purposes; that bed was warm, and the thermometer a long way below freezing; that he was clad but lightly in his slippers, dressing-gown, and nightcap; and that he had a cold upon him at that time. The grasp, though gentle as a woman's hand, was not to be resisted. He rose; but, finding that the Spirit made towards the window, clasped its robe in supplication.

'I am a mortal,' Scrooge remonstrated, 'and liable to fall.'

'Bear but a touch of my hand *there*,' said the Spirit, laying it upon his heart, 'and you shall be upheld in more than this!'

As the words were spoken, they passed through the wall, and stood upon an open country road, with fields on either hand. The city had entirely vanished. Not a vestige of it was to be seen. The darkness and the mist had vanished with it, for it was a clear, cold, winter day, with snow upon the ground.

'Good Heaven!' said Scrooge, clasping his hands together, as he looked about him. 'I was bred in this place. I was a boy here!'

The Spirit gazed upon him mildly. Its gentle touch, though it had been light and instantaneous, appeared still present to the old man's sense of feeling. He was conscious of a thousand odours floating in the air, each one connected with a thousand thoughts, and hopes, and joys, and cares long, long forgotten!

'Your lip is trembling,' said the Ghost. 'And what is that upon your cheek?'

Scrooge muttered, with an unusual catching in his voice, that it was a pimple; and begged the Ghost to lead him where he would.

'You recollect the way?' inquired the Spirit.

'Remember it!' cried Scrooge with fervour; 'I could walk it blindfold.'

'Strange to have forgotten it for so many years!' observed the Ghost. 'Let us go on.'

They walked along the road, Scrooge recognising every gate, and post, and tree, until a little market-town appeared in the distance, with its bridge, its church, and winding river. Some shaggy ponies now were seen trotting towards them with boys upon their backs, who called to other boys in country gigs and carts, driven by farmers. All these boys were in great spirits, and shouted to each other, until the broad fields were so full of merry music, that the crisp air laughed to hear it.

'These are but shadows of the things that have been,' said the Ghost. 'They have no consciousness of us.'

The jocund travellers came on; and as they came, Scrooge knew and named them every one. Why was he rejoiced beyond all bounds to see them? Why did his cold eye glisten, and his heart leap up as they went past? Why was he filled with gladness when he heard them give each other Merry Christmas, as they parted at cross-roads and by-ways for their several homes? What was merry Christmas to Scrooge? Out upon merry Christmas! What good had it ever done to him?

'The school is not quite deserted,' said the Ghost. 'A solitary child, neglected by his friends, is left there still.'

Scrooge said he knew it. And he sobbed.

They left the high-road by a well-remembered lane and soon approached a mansion of dull red brick, with a little weather-cock surmounted cupola on the roof, and a bell hanging in it. It was a large house, but one of broken fortunes; for the spacious offices were little used, their walls were damp and mossy, their windows broken, and their gates decayed. Fowls clucked and strutted in the stables; and the coach-houses and sheds were overrun with grass. Nor was it more retentive of its ancient state within; for, entering the dreary hall, and glancing through the open doors of many rooms, they found them poorly furnished, cold, and vast. There was an earthy savour in the air, a chilly bareness in the place, which associated itself somehow with too much getting up by candle light and not too much to eat.

They went, the Ghost and Scrooge, across the hall, to a door at the back of the house. It opened before them, and disclosed a long, bare, melancholy room, made barer still by lines of plain deal forms and desks. At one of these a lonely boy was reading near a feeble fire; and Scrooge sat down upon a form, and wept to see his poor forgotten self as he had used to be.

Not a latent echo in the house, not a squeak and scuffle from the mice behind the panelling, not a drip from the half-thawed waterspout in the dull yard behind, not a sigh among the leafless boughs of one despondent poplar, not the idle swinging of an empty storehouse door, no, not a clicking in the fire, but fell upon the heart of Scrooge with softening influence, and gave a freer passage to his tears.

The Spirit touched him on the arm, and pointed to his younger self, intent upon his reading. Suddenly a man in foreign garments, wonderfully real and distinct to look at, stood outside the window, with an axe stuck in his belt, and leading by the bridle an ass laden with wood.

'Why, it's Ali Baba!' Scrooge exclaimed in ecstasy. 'It's dear old honest Ali Baba! Yes, yes, I know. One Christmas-time, when yonder solitary child was left here all alone, he *did* come, for the first time, just like that. Poor boy! And Valentine,' said Scrooge, 'and his wild brother, Orson; there they go! And what's his name, who was put down in his drawers, asleep, at the gate of Damascus; don't you see him? And the Sultan's Groom turned upside down by the Genii; there he is upon his head! Serve him right! I'm glad of it. What business had he to be married to the Princess?'

To hear Scrooge expending all the earnestness of his nature on such subjects, in a most extraordinary voice between laughing and crying; and to see his heightened and excited face; would have been a surprise to his business friends in the City, indeed.

'There's the Parrot!' cried Scrooge. 'Green body and yellow tail, with a thing like a lettuce growing out of the top of his head; there he is! Poor Robin Crusoe he called him, when he came home again after sailing round the island. "Poor Robin Crusoe, where have you been, Robin Crusoe?" The man thought he was dreaming, but he wasn't. It was the Parrot, you know. There goes Friday, running for his life to the little creek! Halloa! Hoop! Halloo!'

Then, with a rapidity of transition very foreign to his usual character, he said, in pity for his former self, 'Poor boy!' and cried again.

'I wish,' Scrooge muttered, putting his hand in his pocket, and looking about him, after drying his eyes with his cuff; 'but it's too late now.'

'What is the matter?' asked the Spirit.

'Nothing,' said Scrooge. 'Nothing. There was a boy singing a Christmas carol at my door last night. I should like to have given him something: that's all.'

The Ghost smiled thoughtfully, and waved its hand, saying as it did so, 'Let us see another Christmas!'

Scrooge's former self grew larger at the words, and the room became a little darker and more dirty. The panels shrunk, the windows cracked; fragments of plaster fell out of the ceiling, and the naked laths were shown instead; but how all this was brought about Scrooge knew no more than you do. He only knew that it was quite correct; that everything had happened so; that there he was, alone again, when all the other boys had gone home for the jolly holidays.

He was not reading now, but walking up and down despairingly. Scrooge looked at the Ghost, and, with a mournful shaking of his head, glanced anxiously towards the door.

It opened; and a little girl, much younger than the boy, came darting in, and, putting her arms about his neck, and often kissing him, addressed him as her 'dear, dear brother.'

'I have come to bring you home, dear brother!' said the child, clapping her tiny hands, and bending down to laugh. 'To bring you home, home, home!'

'Home, little Fan?' returned the boy.

'Yes!' said the child, brimful of glee. 'Home for good and all. Home for ever and ever. Father is so much kinder than he used to be, that home's like heaven! He spoke so gently to me one dear night when I was going to bed, that I was not afraid to ask him once more if you might come home; and he said Yes, you should; and sent me in a coach to bring you. And you're to be a man!' said the child, opening her eyes; 'and are never to come back here; but first we're to be together all the Christmas long, and have the merriest time in all the world.'

'You are quite a woman, little Fan!' exclaimed the boy.

She clapped her hands and laughed, and tried to touch his head; but, being too little laughed again, and stood on tiptoe to embrace him. Then she began to drag him, in her childish eagerness, towards the door; and he, nothing loath to go, accompanied her.

A terrible voice in the hall cried, 'Bring down Master Scrooge's box, there!' and in the hall appeared the school-master himself, who glared on Master Scrooge with a ferocious condescension, and threw him into a dreadful state of mind by shaking hands with him. He then conveyed him and his sister into the veriest old well of a shivering best parlour that ever was seen, where the maps upon the wall, and the celestial and terrestrial globes in the windows, were waxy with cold. Here he produced a decanter of curiously light wine, and a block of curiously heavy cake, and administered instalments of those dainties to the young people; at the same time sending out a meagre servant to offer a glass of 'something' to the postboy, who answered that he thanked the gentleman, but, if it was the same tap as he had tasted before, he had rather not. Master Scrooge's trunk being by this time tied on to the top of the chaise, the children bade the schoolmaster good-bye right willingly; and, getting into it, drove gaily down the garden sweep; the quick wheels dashing the hoar-frost and snow from off the dark leaves of the evergreens like spray.

'Always a delicate creature, whom a breath might have withered,' said the Ghost. 'But she had a large heart!'

'So she had,' cried Scrooge. 'You're right. I will not gainsay it, Spirit. God forbid!'

'She died a woman,' said the Ghost, 'and had, as I think, children.'

'One child,' Scrooge returned.

'True,' said the Ghost. 'Your nephew!'

Scrooge seemed uneasy in his mind, and answered briefly, 'Yes.'

Although they had but that moment left the school behind them, they were now in the busy thoroughfares of a city, where shadowy passengers passed and re-passed; where shadowy carts and coaches battled for the way, and all the strife and tumult of a real city were. It was made plain enough, by the dressing of the shops, that here, too, it was Christmas-time again; but it was evening, and the streets were lighted up.

The Ghost stopped at a certain warehouse door, and asked Scrooge if he knew it.

'Know it!' said Scrooge. 'Was I apprenticed here?'

They went in. At sight of an old gentleman in a Welsh wig, sitting behind such a high desk, that if he had been two inches taller, he must have knocked his head against the ceiling, Scrooge cried in great excitement—

'Why, it's old Fezziwig! Bless his heart, it's Fezziwig alive again!'

Old Fezziwig laid down his pen, and looked up at the clock, which pointed to the hour of seven. He rubbed his hands; adjusted his capacious waistcoat; laughed all over himself, from his shoes to his organ of benevolence; and called out, in a comfortable, oily, rich, fat, jovial voice—

'Yo ho, there! Ebenezer! Dick!'

Scrooge's former self, now grown a young man, came briskly in, accompanied by his fellow-'prentice.

'Dick Wilkins, to be sure!' said Scrooge to the Ghost. 'Bless me, yes. There he is. He was very much attached to me, was Dick. Poor Dick! Dear, dear!'

'Yo ho, my boys!' said Fezziwig. 'No more work to-night. Christmas Eve, Dick. Christmas, Ebenezer! Let's have the shutters up,' cried old Fezziwig, with a sharp clap of his hands, 'before a man can say Jack Robinson!'

You wouldn't believe how those two fellows went at it! They charged into the street with the shutters—one, two, three—had 'em up in their places—four, five, six—barred 'em and pinned 'em—seven, eight, nine—and came back before you could have got to twelve, panting like racehorses.

'Hilli-ho!' cried old Fezziwig, skipping down from the high desk with wonderful agility. 'Clear away, my lads, and let's have lots of room here! Hilli-ho, Dick! Chirrup, Ebenezer!'

Clear away! There was nothing they wouldn't have cleared away, or couldn't have cleared away, with old Fezziwig looking on. It was done in a minute. Every movable was packed off, as if it were dismissed from public life for evermore; the floor was swept and watered, the lamps were trimmed, fuel was heaped upon the fire; and the warehouse was as snug, and warm, and dry, and bright a ball-room as you would desire to see upon a winter's night.

In came a fiddler with a music-book, and went up to the lofty desk, and made an orchestra of it, and tuned like fifty stomach-aches. In came Mrs. Fezziwig, one vast substantial smile. In came the three Miss Fezziwigs, beaming and lovable. In came the six young followers whose hearts they broke. In came all the young men and women employed in the business. In came the housemaid, with her cousin the baker. In came the cook with her brother's particular friend the milkman. In came the boy from over the way, who was suspected of not having board enough from his master; trying to hide himself behind the girl from next door but one, who was proved to have had her ears pulled by her mistress. In they all came, one after another; some shyly, some boldly, some gracefully, some awkwardly, some pushing, some pulling; in they all came, any how and every how. Away they all went, twenty couple at once; hands half round and back again the other way; down the middle and up again; round and round in various stages of affectionate grouping; old top couple always turning up in the wrong place; new top couple starting off again as soon as they got there; all top couples at last, and not a bottom one to help them! When this result was brought about, old Fezziwig, clapping his hands to stop the dance, cried out, 'Well done!' and the fiddler plunged his hot face into a pot of porter, especially provided for that purpose. But, scorning rest upon his reappearance, he instantly began again, though there were no dancers yet, as if the other fiddler had been carried home, exhausted, on a shutter, and he were a bran-new man resolved to beat him out of sight, or perish.

There were more dances, and there were forfeits, and more dances, and there was cake, and there was negus, and there was a great piece of Cold Roast, and there was a great piece of Cold Boiled, and there were mince-pies, and plenty of beer. But the great effect of the evening came after the Roast and Boiled, when the fiddler (an artful dog, mind! The sort of man who knew his business better than you or I could have told it him!) struck up 'Sir Roger de Coverley.' Then old Fezziwig stood out to dance with Mrs. Fezziwig. Top couple, too; with a good stiff piece of work cut out for them; three or four and twenty pair of partners; people who were not to be trifled with; people who would dance, and had no notion of walking.

But if they had been twice as many—ah! four times—old Fezziwig would have been a match for them, and so would Mrs. Fezziwig. As to *her*, she was worthy to be his partner in every sense of the term. If that's not high praise, tell me higher, and I'll use it. A positive light appeared to issue from Fezziwig's calves. They shone in every part of the dance like moons. You couldn't have predicted, at any given time, what would become of them next. And when old Fezziwig and Mrs. Fezziwig had gone all through the dance; advance and retire, both hands to your partner, bow and curtsy, cork-screw, thread-the-needle, and back again to your place: Fezziwig 'cut'—cut so deftly, that he appeared to wink with his legs, and came upon his feet again without a stagger.

When the clock struck eleven, this domestic ball broke up. Mr. and Mrs. Fezziwig took their stations, one on either side the door, and, shaking hands with every person individu-ally as he or she went out, wished him or her a Merry Christmas. When everybody had retired but the two 'prentices, they did the same to them; and thus the cheerful voices died away, and the lads were left to their beds; which were under a counter in the back-shop.

During the whole of this time Scrooge had acted like a man out of his wits. His heart and soul were in the scene, and with his former self. He corroborated everything, remembered everything, enjoyed everything, and underwent the strangest agitation. It was not until now, when the bright faces of his former self and Dick were turned from them, that he remembered the Ghost, and became conscious that it was looking full upon him, while the light upon its head burnt very clear.

'A small matter,' said the Ghost, 'to make these silly folks so full of gratitude.'

'Small!' echoed Scrooge.

The Spirit signed to him to listen to the two apprentices, who were pouring out their hearts in praise of Fezziwig; and when he had done so, said:

'Why! Is it not? He has spent but a few pounds of your mortal money: three or four, perhaps. Is that so much that he deserves this praise?'

'It isn't that,' said Scrooge, heated by the remark, and speaking unconsciously like his former, not his latter self. 'It isn't that, Spirit. He has the power to render us happy or unhappy; to make our service light or burdensome; a pleasure or a toil. Say that his power lies in words and looks; in things so slight and insignificant that it is impossible to add and count 'em up: what then? The happiness he gives is quite as great as if it cost a fortune.'

He felt the Spirit's glance, and stopped.

'What is the matter?' asked the Ghost.

'Nothing particular,' said Scrooge.

'Something, I think?' the Ghost insisted.

'No,' said Scrooge, 'no. I should like to be able to say a word or two to my clerk just now. That's all.'

His former self turned down the lamps as he gave utterance to the wish; and Scrooge and the Ghost again stood side by side in the open air.

'My time grows short,' observed the Spirit. 'Quick!'

This was not addressed to Scrooge, or to any one whom he could see, but it produced an immediate effect. For again Scrooge saw himself. He was older now; a man in the prime of life. His face had not the harsh and rigid lines of later years; but it had begun to wear the signs of care and avarice. There was an eager, greedy, restless motion in the eye, which showed the passion that had taken root, and where the shadow of the growing tree would fall.

He was not alone, but sat by the side of a fair young girl in a mourning dress: in whose eyes there were tears, which sparkled in the light that shone out of the Ghost of Christmas Past.

'It matters little,' she said softly. 'To you, very little. Another idol has displaced me; and, if it can cheer and comfort you in time to come as I would have tried to do, I have no just cause to grieve.'

'What Idol has displaced you?' he rejoined.

'A golden one.'

'This is the even-handed dealing of the world!' he said. 'There is nothing on which it is so hard as poverty; and there is nothing it professes to condemn with such severity as the pursuit of wealth!'

'You fear the world too much,' she answered gently. 'All your other hopes have merged into the hope of being beyond the chance of its sordid reproach. I have seen your nobler aspirations fall off one by one, until the master passion, Gain, engrosses you. Have I not?'

'What then?' he retorted. 'Even if I have grown so much wiser, what then? I am not changed towards you.'

She shook her head.

'Am I?'

'Our contract is an old one. It was made when we were both poor, and content to be so, until, in good season, we could improve our worldly fortune by our patient industry. You *are* changed. When it was made you were another man.'

'I was a boy,' he said impatiently.

'Your own feeling tells you that you were not what you are,' she returned. 'I am. That which promised happiness when we were one in heart is fraught with misery now that we are two. How often and how keenly I have thought of this I will not say. It is enough that I *have* thought of it, and can release you.'

'Have I ever sought release?'

'In words. No. Never.'

'In what, then?'

'In a changed nature; in an altered spirit; in another atmosphere of life; another Hope as its great end. In every-thing that made my love of any worth or value in your sight. If this had never been between us,' said the girl, looking mildly, but with steadiness, upon him; 'tell me, would you seek me out and try to win me now? Ah, no!'

He seemed to yield to the justice of this supposition in spite of himself. But he said, with a struggle, 'You think not.'

'I would gladly think otherwise if I could,' she answered. 'Heaven knows! When *I* have learned a Truth like this, I know how strong and irresistible it must be. But if you were free to-day, to-morrow, yesterday, can even I believe that you would choose a dowerless girl—you who, in your very confidence with her, weigh everything by Gain: or, choosing her, if for a moment you were false enough to your one guiding principle to do so, do I not know that your repentance and regret would surely follow? I do; and I release you. With a full heart, for the love of him you once were.'

He was about to speak; but, with her head turned from him, she resumed:

'You may—the memory of what is past half makes me hope you will—have pain in this. A very, very brief time, and you will dismiss the recollection of it gladly, as an unprofitable dream, from which it happened well that you awoke. May you be happy in the life you have chosen!'

She left him, and they parted.

'Spirit!' said Scrooge, 'show me no more! Conduct me home. Why do you delight to torture me?'

'One shadow more!' exclaimed the Ghost.

'No more!' cried Scrooge. 'No more! I don't wish to see it. Show me no more!'

But the relentless Ghost pinioned him in both his arms, and forced him to observe what happened next.

They were in another scene and place; a room, not very large or handsome, but full of comfort. Near to the winter fire sat a beautiful young girl, so like that last that Scrooge believed it was the same, until he saw *her*, now a comely matron, sitting opposite her daughter. The noise in this room was perfectly tumultuous, for there were more children there than Scrooge in his agitated state of mind could count; and, unlike the celebrated herd in the poem, they were not forty children conducting themselves like one, but every child was conducting itself like forty. The consequences were uproarious beyond belief; but no one seemed to care; on the contrary, the mother and daughter laughed heartily, and enjoyed it very much; and the latter, soon beginning to mingle in the sports, got pillaged by the young brigands most ruthlessly. What would I not have given to be one of them! Though I never could have been so rude, no, no! I wouldn't for the wealth of all the world have crushed that braided hair, and torn it down; and for the precious little shoe, I wouldn't have plucked it off, God bless my soul! to save my life. As to measuring her waist in sport, as they did, bold young brood, I couldn't have done it; I should have expected my arm to have grown round it for a punishment, and never come straight again. And yet I should have dearly liked, I own, to have touched her lips; to have questioned her, that she might have opened them; to have looked upon the lashes of her downcast eyes, and never raised a blush; to have let loose waves of hair, an inch of which would be a keepsake beyond price: in short, I should have liked, I do confess, to have had the lightest license of a child, and yet to have been man enough to know its value.

But now a knocking at the door was heard, and such a rush immediately ensued that she, with laughing face and plundered dress, was borne towards it the centre of a flushed and boisterous group, just in time to greet the father, who came home attended by a man laden with Christmas toys and presents. Then the shouting and the struggling, and the onslaught that was made on the defenceless porter! The scaling him, with chairs for ladders, to dive into his pockets, despoil him of brown-paper parcels, hold on tight by his cravat, hug him round his neck, pummel his back, and kick his legs in irrepressible affection! The shouts of wonder and delight with which the development of every package was received! The terrible announcement that the baby had been taken in the act of putting a doll's frying pan into his mouth, and was more than suspected of having swallowed a fictitious turkey, glued on a wooden platter! The immense relief of finding this a false alarm! The joy, and gratitude, and ecstasy! They are all indescribable alike. It is enough that, by degrees, the children and their emotions got out of the parlour, and, by one stair at a time, up to the top of the house, where they went to bed, and so subsided.

And now Scrooge looked on more attentively than ever, when the master of the house, having his daughter leaning fondly on him, sat down with her and her mother at his own fireside; and when he thought that such another creature, quite as graceful and as full of promise, might have called him father, and been a spring-time in the haggard winter of his life, his sight grew very dim indeed.

'Belle,' said the husband, turning to his wife with a smile, 'I saw an old friend of yours this afternoon.'

'Who was it?'

'Guess!'

'How can I? Tut, don't I know?' she added in the same breath, laughing as he laughed. 'Mr. Scrooge.'

'Mr. Scrooge it was. I passed his office window; and as it was not shut up, and he had a candle inside, I could scarcely help seeing him. His partner lies upon the point of death, I hear; and there he sat alone. Quite alone in the world, I do believe.'

'Spirit!' said Scrooge in a broken voice, 'remove me from this place.'

'I told you these were shadows of the things that have been,' said the Ghost. 'That they are what they are do not blame me!'

'Remove me!' Scrooge exclaimed, 'I cannot bear it!'

He turned upon the Ghost, and seeing that it looked upon him with a face, in which in some strange way there were fragments of all the faces it had shown him, wrestled with it.

'Leave me! Take me back. Haunt me no longer!'

In the struggle, if that can be called a struggle in which the Ghost with no visible resistance on its own part was undisturbed by any effort of its adversary, Scrooge observed that its light was burning high and bright; and dimly connecting that with its influence over him, he seized the extinguisher-cap, and by a sudden action pressed it down upon its head.

The Spirit dropped beneath it, so that the extinguisher covered its whole form; but though Scrooge pressed it down with all his force, he could not hide the light, which streamed from under it, in an unbroken flood upon the ground.

He was conscious of being exhausted, and overcome by an irresistible drowsiness; and, further, of being in his own bedroom. He gave the cap a parting squeeze, in which his hand relaxed; and had barely time to reel to bed, before he sank into a heavy sleep.

STAVE THREE

## The Second of the Three Spirits

AWAKING IN THE MIDDLE OF A PRODIGIOUSLY tough snore, and sitting up in bed to get his thoughts together, Scrooge had no occasion to be told that the bell was again upon the stroke of One. He felt that he was restored to consciousness in the right nick of time, for the especial purpose of holding a conference with the second messenger despatched to him through Jacob Marley's intervention. But finding that he turned uncomfortably cold when he began to wonder which of his curtains this new spectre would draw back, he put them every one aside with his own hands, and, lying down again, established a sharp look-out all round the bed. For he wished to challenge the Spirit on the moment of its appearance, and did not wish to be taken by surprise and made nervous.

Gentlemen of the free-and-easy sort, who plume themselves on being acquainted with a move or two, and being usually equal to the time of day, express the wide range of their capacity for adventure by observing that they are good for anything from pitch-and-toss to manslaughter; between which opposite extremes, no doubt, there lies a tolerably wide and comprehensive range of subjects. Without venturing for Scrooge quite as hardily as this, I don't mind calling on you to believe that he was ready for a good broad field of strange appearances, and that nothing between a baby and a rhinoceros would have astonished him very much.

Now, being prepared for almost anything, he was not by any means prepared for nothing; and consequently, when the bell struck One, and no shape appeared, he was taken with a violent fit of trembling. Five minutes, ten minutes, a quarter of an hour went by, yet nothing came. All this time he lay upon his bed, the very core and centre of a blaze of ruddy light, which streamed upon it when the clock proclaimed the hour; and which, being only light, was more alarming than a dozen ghosts, as he was powerless to make out what it meant, or would be at; and was sometimes apprehensive that he might be at that very moment an interesting case of spontaneous combustion, without having the consolation of knowing it. At last, however, he began to think—as you or I would have thought at first; for it is always the person not in the predicament who knows what ought to have been done in it, and would unquestionably have done it too—at last, I say, he began to think that the source and secret of this ghostly light might be in the adjoining room, from whence, on further tracing it, it seemed to shine. This idea taking full possession of his mind, he got up softly, and shuffled in his slippers to the door.

The moment Scrooge's hand was on the lock a strange voice called him by his name, and bade him enter. He obeyed.

Scrooge's third Visitor.

London Chapman & Hall 186 Strand.

It was his own room. There was no doubt about that. But it had undergone a surprising transformation. The walls and ceiling were so hung with living green, that it looked a perfect grove; from every part of which bright gleaming berries glistened. The crisp leaves of holly, mistletoe, and ivy reflected back the light, as if so many little mirrors had been scattered there; and such a mighty blaze went roaring up the chimney as that dull petrification of a hearth had never known in Scrooge's time, or Marley's, or for many and many a winter season gone. Heaped up on the floor, to form a kind of throne, were turkeys, geese, game, poultry, brawn, great joints of meat, sucking-pigs, long wreaths of sausages, mince-pies, plum-puddings, barrels of oysters, red-hot chestnuts, cherry-cheeked apples, juicy oranges, luscious pears, immense twelfth-cakes, and seething bowls of punch, that made the chamber dim with their delicious steam. In easy state upon this couch there sat a jolly Giant, glorious to see; who bore a glowing torch, in shape not unlike Plenty's horn, and held it up, high up, to shed its light on Scrooge as he came peeping round the door.

'Come in!' exclaimed the Ghost. 'Come in! and know me better, man!'

Scrooge entered timidly, and hung his head before this Spirit. He was not the dogged Scrooge he had been; and though the Spirit's eyes were clear and kind, he did not like to meet them.

'I am the Ghost of Christmas Present,' said the Spirit. 'Look upon me!'

Scrooge reverently did so. It was clothed in one simple deep green robe, or mantle, bordered with white fur. This garment hung so loosely on the figure, that its capacious breast was bare, as if disdaining to be warded or concealed by any artifice. Its feet, observable beneath the ample folds of the garment, were also bare; and on its head it wore no other covering than a holly wreath, set here and there with shining icicles. Its dark-brown curls were long and free; free as its genial face, its sparkling eye, its open hand, its cheery voice, its unconstrained demeanour, and its joyful air. Girded round its middle was an antique scabbard: but no sword was in it, and the ancient sheath was eaten up with rust.

'You have never seen the like of me before!' exclaimed the Spirit.

'Never,' Scrooge made answer to it.

'Have never walked forth with the younger members of my family; meaning (for I am very young) my elder brothers born in these later years?' pursued the Phantom.

'I don't think I have,' said Scrooge. 'I am afraid I have not. Have you had many brothers, Spirit?'

'More than eighteen hundred,' said the Ghost.

'A tremendous family to provide for,' muttered Scrooge.

The Ghost of Christmas Present rose.

'Spirit,' said Scrooge submissively, 'conduct me where you will. I went forth last night on compulsion, and I learned a lesson which is working now. To-night if you have aught to teach me, let me profit by it.'

'Touch my robe!'

Scrooge did as he was told, and held it fast.

Holly, mistletoe, red berries, ivy, turkeys, geese, game, poultry, brawn, meat, pigs, sausages, oysters, pies, puddings, fruit, and punch, all vanished instantly. So did the room, the fire, the ruddy glow, the hour of night, and they stood in the city streets on Christmas morning, where (for the weather was severe) the people made a rough, but brisk and not unpleasant kind of music, in scraping the snow from the pavement in front of their dwellings, and from the tops of their houses, whence it was mad delight to the boys to see it come plumping down into the road below, and splitting into artificial little snowstorms.

The house-fronts looked black enough, and the windows blacker, contrasting with the smooth white sheet of snow upon the roofs, and with the dirtier snow upon the ground; which last deposit had been ploughed up in deep furrows by the heavy wheels of carts and waggons: furrows that crossed and recrossed each other hundreds of times where the great streets branched off; and made intricate channels, hard to trace in the thick yellow mud and icy water. The sky was gloomy, and the shortest streets were choked up with a dingy mist, half thawed, half frozen, whose heavier particles descended in a shower of sooty atoms, as if all the chimneys in Great Britain had, by one consent, caught fire, and were blazing away to their dear heart's content. There was nothing very cheerful in the climate or the town, and yet was there an air of cheerfulness abroad that the clearest summer air and brightest summer sun might have endeavoured to diffuse in vain.

For the people who were shovelling away on the house-tops were jovial and full of glee; calling out to one another from the parapets, and now and then exchanging a facetious snowball—better-natured missile far than many a wordy jest —laughing heartily if it went right, and not less heartily if it went wrong. The poulterers' shops were still half open, and the fruiterers' were radiant in their glory. There were great, round, pot-bellied baskets of chestnuts, shaped like the waistcoats of jolly old gentlemen, lolling at the doors, and tumbling out into the street in their apoplectic opulence: There were ruddy, brown-faced, broad-girthed Spanish onions, shining in the fatness of their growth like Spanish friars, and winking from their shelves in wanton slyness at the girls as they went by, and glanced demurely at the hung-up mistletoe. There were pears and apples clustered high in blooming pyramids; there were bunches of grapes, made, in the shopkeepers' benevolence, to dangle from conspicuous hooks that people's mouths might water gratis as they passed; there were piles of filberts, mossy and brown, recalling, in their fragrance, ancient walks among the woods, and pleasant shufflings ankle deep through withered leaves; there were Norfolk Biffins, squab and swarthy, setting off the yellow of the oranges and lemons, and, in the great compactness of their juicy persons, urgently entreating and beseeching to be carried home in paper bags and eaten after dinner. The very gold and silver fish, set forth among these choice fruits in a bowl, though members of a dull and stagnant-blooded race, appeared to know that there was something going on; and, to a fish, went gasping round and round their little world in slow and passionless excitement.

The Grocers'! oh, the Grocers'! nearly closed, with perhaps two shutters down, or one; but through those gaps such glimpses! It was not alone that the scales descending on the counter made a merry sound, or that the twine and roller parted company so briskly, or that the canisters were rattled up and down like juggling tricks, or even that the blended scents of tea and coffee were so grateful to the nose, or even that the raisins were so plentiful and rare, the almonds so extremely white, the sticks of cinnamon so long and straight, the other spices so delicious, the candied fruits so caked and spotted with molten sugar as to make the coldest lookers-on feel faint, and subsequently bilious. Nor was it that the figs were moist and pulpy, or that the French plums blushed in modest tartness from their highly-decorated boxes, or that everything was good to eat and in its Christmas dress; but the customers were all so hurried and so eager in the hopeful promise of the day, that they tumbled up against each other at the door, crashing their wicker baskets wildly, and left their purchases upon the counter, and came running back to fetch them, and committed hundreds of the like mistakes, in the best humour possible; while the grocer and his people were so frank and fresh, that the polished hearts with which they fastened their aprons behind might have been their own, worn outside for general inspection, and for Christmas daws to peck at if they chose.

But soon the steeples called good people all to church and chapel, and away they came, flocking through the streets in their best clothes and with their gayest faces. And at the same time there emerged, from scores of by-streets, lanes, and nameless turnings, innumerable people, carrying their dinners to the bakers' shops. The sight of these poor revellers appeared to interest the Spirit very much, for he stood with Scrooge beside him in a baker's doorway, and, taking off the covers as their bearers passed, sprinkled incense on their dinners from his torch. And it was a very uncommon kind of torch, for once or twice, when there were angry words between some dinner-carriers who had jostled each other, he shed a few drops of water on them from it, and their good-humour was restored directly. For they said, it was a shame to quarrel upon Christmas Day. And so it was! God love it, so it was!

In time the bells ceased, and the bakers were shut up; and yet there was a genial shadowing forth of all these dinners, and the progress of their cooking, in the thawed blotch of wet above each baker's oven, where the pavement smoked as if its stones were cooking too.

'Is there a peculiar flavour in what you sprinkle from your torch?' asked Scrooge.

'There is. My own.'

'Would it apply to any kind of dinner on this day?' asked Scrooge.

'To any kindly given. To a poor one most.'

'Why to a poor one most?' asked Scrooge.

'Because it needs it most.'

'Spirit!' said Scrooge, after a moment's thought, 'I wonder you, of all the beings in the many worlds about us, should desire to cramp these people's opportunities of innocent enjoyment.'

'I!' cried the Spirit.

'You would deprive them of their means of dining every seventh day, often the only day on which they can be said to dine at all,' said Scrooge; 'wouldn't you?'

'I!' cried the Spirit.

'You seek to close these places on the Seventh Day,' said Scrooge. 'And it comes to the same thing.'

'I seek!' exclaimed the Spirit.

'Forgive me if I am wrong. It has been done in your name, or at least in that of your family,' said Scrooge.

'There are some upon this earth of yours,' returned the Spirit, 'who lay claim to know us, and who do their deeds of passion, pride, ill-will, hatred, envy, bigotry, and selfishness in our name, who are as strange to us, and all our kith and kin, as if they had never lived. Remember that, and charge their doings on themselves, not us.'

Scrooge promised that he would; and they went on, invisible, as they had been before, into the suburbs of the town. It was a remarkable quality of the Ghost (which Scrooge had observed at the baker's), that notwithstanding his gigantic size, he could accommodate himself to any place with ease; and that he stood beneath a low roof quite as gracefully and like a supernatural creature as it was possible he could have done in any lofty hall.

And perhaps it was the pleasure the good Spirit had in showing off this power of his, or else it was his own kind, generous, hearty nature, and his sympathy with all poor men, that led him straight to Scrooge's clerk's; for there he went, and took Scrooge with him, holding to his robe; and on the threshold of the door the Spirit smiled, and stopped to bless Bob Cratchit's dwelling with the sprinklings of his torch. Think of that! Bob had but fifteen 'Bob' a week himself; he pocketed on Saturdays but fifteen copies of his Christian name; and yet the Ghost of Christmas Present blessed his four-roomed house!

Then up rose Mrs. Cratchit, Cratchit's wife, dressed out but poorly in a twice-turned gown, but brave in ribbons, which are cheap, and make a goodly show for sixpence; and she laid the cloth, assisted by Belinda Cratchit, second of her daughters, also brave in ribbons; while Master Peter Cratchit plunged a fork into the saucepan of potatoes, and getting the corners of his monstrous shirt-collar (Bob's private property, conferred upon his son and heir in honour of the day,) into his mouth, rejoiced to find himself so gallantly attired, and yearned to show his linen in the fashionable Parks. And now two smaller Cratchits, boy and girl, came tearing in, screaming that outside the baker's they had smelt the goose, and known it for their own; and basking in luxurious thoughts of sage and onion, these young Cratchits danced about the table, and exalted Master Peter Cratchit to the skies, while he (not proud, although his collars nearly choked him) blew the fire, until the slow potatoes, bubbling up, knocked loudly at the saucepan-lid to be let out and peeled.

'What has ever got your precious father, then?' said Mrs. Cratchit. 'And your brother, Tiny Tim? And Martha warn't as late last Christmas Day by half an hour!'

'Here's Martha, mother!' said a girl, appearing as she spoke.

'Here's Martha, mother!' cried the two young Cratchits. 'Hurrah! There's *such* a goose, Martha!'

'Why, bless your heart alive, my dear, how late you are!' said Mrs. Cratchit, kissing her a dozen times, and taking off her shawl and bonnet for her with officious zeal.

'We'd a deal of work to finish up last night,' replied the girl, 'and had to clear away this morning, mother!'

'Well! never mind so long as you are come,' said Mrs. Cratchit. 'Sit ye down before the fire, my dear, and have a warm, Lord bless ye!'

'No, no! There's father coming,' cried the two young Cratchits, who were everywhere at once. 'Hide, Martha, hide!'

So Martha hid herself, and in came little Bob, the father, with at least three feet of comforter, exclusive of the fringe, hanging down before him, and his threadbare clothes darned up and brushed to look seasonable, and Tiny Tim upon his shoulder. Alas for Tiny Tim, he bore a little crutch, and had his limbs supported by an iron frame!

'Why, where's our Martha?' cried Bob Cratchit, looking round.

'Not coming,' said Mrs. Cratchit.

'Not coming!' said Bob, with a sudden declension in his high spirits; for he had been Tim's blood-horse all the way from church, and had come home rampant. 'Not coming upon Christmas Day!'

Martha didn't like to see him disappointed, if it were only in joke; so she came out prematurely from behind the closet door, and ran into his arms, while the two young Cratchits hustled Tiny Tim, and bore him off into the wash-house, that he might hear the pudding singing in the copper.

'And how did little Tim behave?' asked Mrs. Cratchit when she had rallied Bob on his credulity, and Bob had hugged his daughter to his heart's content.

'As good as gold,' said Bob, 'and better. Somehow, he gets thoughtful, sitting by himself so much, and thinks the strangest things you ever heard. He told me, coming home, that he hoped the people saw him in the church, because he was a cripple, and it might be pleasant to them to remember upon Christmas Day who made lame beggars walk and blind men see.'

Bob's voice was tremulous when he told them this, and trembled more when he said that Tiny Tim was growing strong and hearty.

His active little crutch was heard upon the floor, and back came Tiny Tim before another word was spoken, escorted by his brother and sister to his stool beside the fire; and while Bob, turning up his cuffs—as if, poor fellow, they were capable of being made more shabby—compounded some hot mixture in a jug with gin and lemons, and stirred it round and round, and put it on the hob to simmer, Master Peter and the two ubiquitous young Cratchits went to fetch the goose, with which they soon returned in high procession.

Such a bustle ensued that you might have thought a goose the rarest of all birds; a feathered phenomenon, to which a black swan was a matter of course—and, in truth, it was something very like it in that house. Mrs. Cratchit made the gravy (ready beforehand in a little saucepan) hissing hot; Master Peter mashed the potatoes with incredible vigour; Miss Belinda sweetened up the apple sauce; Martha dusted the hot plates; Bob took Tiny Tim beside him in a tiny corner at the table; the two young Cratchits set chairs for everybody, not forgetting themselves, and, mounting guard upon their posts, crammed spoons into their mouths, lest they should shriek for goose before their turn came to be helped. At last the dishes were set on, and grace was said. It was succeeded by a breathless pause, as Mrs. Cratchit, looking slowly all along the carving-knife, prepared to plunge it in the breast; but when she did, and when the long-expected gush of stuffing issued forth, one murmur of delight arose all round the board, and even Tiny Tim, excited by the two young Cratchits, beat on the table with the handle of his knife and feebly cried Hurrah!

There never was such a goose. Bob said he didn't believe there ever was such a goose cooked. Its tenderness and flavour, size and cheapness, were the themes of universal admiration. Eked out by apple sauce and mashed potatoes, it was a sufficient dinner for the whole family; indeed, as Mrs. Cratchit said with great delight (surveying one small atom of a bone upon the dish), they hadn't ate it all at last! Yet every one had had enough, and the youngest Cratchits, in particular, were steeped in sage and onion to the eyebrows! But now, the plates being changed by Miss Belinda, Mrs. Cratchit left the room alone—too nervous to bear witnesses—to take the pudding up, and bring it in.

Suppose it should not be done enough! Suppose it should break in turning out! Suppose somebody should have got over the wall of the back-yard and stolen it, while they were merry with the goose—a supposition at which the two young Cratchits became livid! All sorts of horrors were supposed.

Hallo! A great deal of steam! The pudding was out of the copper. A smell like a washing-day! That was the cloth. A smell like an eating-house and a pastry-cook's next door to each other, with a laundress's next door to that! That was the pudding! In half a minute Mrs. Cratchit entered—flushed, but smiling proudly—with the pudding, like a speckled cannon-ball, so hard and firm, blazing in half of half-a-quartern of ignited brandy, and bedight with Christmas holly stuck into the top.

Oh, a wonderful pudding! Bob Cratchit said, and calmly too, that he regarded it as the greatest success achieved by Mrs. Cratchit since their marriage. Mrs. Cratchit said that, now the weight was off her mind, she would confess she had her doubts about the quantity of flour. Everybody had something to say about it, but nobody said or thought it was at all a small pudding for a large family. It would have been flat heresy to do so. Any Cratchit would have blushed to hint at such a thing.

At last the dinner was all done, the cloth was cleared, the hearth swept, and the fire made up. The compound in the jug being tasted and considered perfect, apples and oranges were put upon the table, and a shovel full of chestnuts on the fire. Then all the Cratchit family drew round the hearth in what Bob Cratchit called a circle, meaning half a one; and at Bob Cratchit's elbow stood the family display of glass. Two tumblers and a custard cup without a handle.

These held the hot stuff from the jug, however, as well as golden goblets would have done; and Bob served it out with beaming looks, while the chestnuts on the fire sputtered and cracked noisily. Then Bob proposed:

'A merry Christmas to us all, my dears. God bless us!'

Which all the family re-echoed.

'God bless us every one!' said Tiny Tim, the last of all.

He sat very close to his father's side, upon his little stool. Bob held his withered little hand to his, as if he loved the child, and wished to keep him by his side, and dreaded that he might be taken from him.

'Spirit,' said Scrooge, with an interest he had never felt before, 'tell me if Tiny Tim will live.'

'I see a vacant seat,' replied the Ghost, 'in the poor chimney corner, and a crutch without an owner, carefully preserved. If these shadows remain unaltered by the Future, the child will die.'

'No, no,' said Scrooge. 'Oh no, kind Spirit! say he will be spared.'

'If these shadows remain unaltered by the Future none other of my race,' returned the Ghost, 'will find him here. What then? If he be like to die, he had better do it, and decrease the surplus population.'

Scrooge hung his head to hear his own words quoted by the Spirit, and was overcome with penitence and grief.

'Man,' said the Ghost, 'if man you be in heart, not adamant, forbear that wicked cant until you have discovered what the surplus is, and where it is. Will you decide what men shall live, what men shall die? It may be that, in the sight of Heaven, you are more worthless and less fit to live than millions like this poor man's child. O God! to hear the insect on the leaf pronouncing on the too much life among his hungry brothers in the dust!'

Scrooge bent before the Ghost's rebuke, and, trembling, cast his eyes upon the ground. But he raised them speedily on hearing his own name.

'Mr. Scrooge!' said Bob. 'I'll give you Mr. Scrooge, the Founder of the Feast!'

'The Founder of the Feast, indeed!' cried Mrs. Cratchit, reddening. 'I wish I had him here. I'd give him a piece of my mind to feast upon, and I hope he'd have a good appetite for it.'

'My dear,' said Bob, 'the children! Christmas Day.'

'It should be Christmas Day, I am sure,' said she, 'on which one drinks the health of such an odious, stingy, hard, unfeeling man as Mr. Scrooge. You know he is, Robert! Nobody knows it better than you do, poor fellow!'

'My dear!' was Bob's mild answer. 'Christmas Day.'

'I'll drink his health for your sake and the Day's,' said Mrs. Cratchit, 'not for his. Long life to him! A merry Christmas and a happy New Year! He'll be very merry and very happy, I have no doubt!'

The children drank the toast after her. It was the first of their proceedings which had no heartiness in it. Tiny Tim drank it last of all, but he didn't care twopence for it. Scrooge was the Ogre of the family. The mention of his name cast a dark shadow on the party, which was not dispelled for full five minutes.

After it had passed away they were ten times merrier than before, from the mere relief of Scrooge the Baleful being done with. Bob Cratchit told them how he had a situation in his eye for Master Peter, which would bring in, if obtained, full five-and-sixpence weekly. The two young Cratchits laughed tremendously at the idea of Peter's being a man of business; and Peter himself looked thoughtfully at the fire from between his collars, as if he were deliberating what particular investments he should favour when he came into the receipt of that bewildering income. Martha, who was a poor apprentice at a milliner's, then told them what kind of work she had to do, and how many hours she worked at a stretch and how she meant to lie abed to-morrow morning for a good long rest; to-morrow being a holiday she passed at home. Also how she had seen a countess and a lord some days before, and how the lord 'was much about as tall as Peter'; at which Peter pulled up his collar so high that you couldn't have seen his head if you had been there. All this time the chestnuts and the jug went round and round; and by-and-by they had a song, about a lost child travelling in the snow, from Tiny Tim, who had a plaintive little voice, and sang it very well indeed.

There was nothing of high mark in this. They were not a handsome family; they were not well dressed; their shoes were far from being waterproof; their clothes were scanty; and Peter might have known, and very likely did, the inside of a pawnbroker's. But they were happy, grateful, pleased with one another, and contented with the time; and when they faded, and looked happier yet in the bright sprinklings of the Spirit's torch at parting, Scrooge had his eye upon them, and especially on Tiny Tim, until the last.

By this time it was getting dark, and snowing pretty heavily; and as Scrooge and the Spirit went along the streets, the brightness of the roaring fires in kitchens, parlours, and all sorts of rooms was wonderful. Here, the flickering of the blaze showed preparations for a cosy dinner, with hot plates baking through and through before the fire, and deep red curtains, ready to be drawn to shut out cold and darkness. There, all the children of the house were running out into the snow to meet their married sisters, brothers, cousins, uncles, aunts, and be the first to greet them. Here, again, were shadows on the window-blinds of guests assembling; and there a group of handsome girls, all hooded and fur-booted, and all chattering at once, tripped lightly off to some near neighbour's house; where, woe upon the single man who saw them enter—artful witches, well they knew it—in a glow!

But, if you had judged from the numbers of people on their way to friendly gatherings, you might have thought that no one was at home to give them welcome when they got there, instead of every house expecting company, and piling up its fires half-chimney high. Blessings on it, how the Ghost exulted! How it bared its breadth of breast, and opened its capacious palm, and floated on, outpouring with a generous hand its bright and harmless mirth on everything within its reach! The very lamplighter, who ran on before, dotting the dusky street with specks of light, and who was dressed to spend the evening somewhere, laughed out loudly as the Spirit passed, though little kenned the lamplighter that he had any company but Christmas.

And now, without a word of warning from the Ghost, they stood upon a bleak and desert moor, where monstrous masses of rude stone were cast about, as though it were the burial-place of giants; and water spread itself wheresoever it listed; or would have done so, but for the frost that held it prisoner; and nothing grew but moss and furze, and coarse, rank grass. Down in the west the setting sun had left a streak of fiery red, which glared upon the desolation for an instant, like a sullen eye, and frowning lower, lower, lower yet, was lost in the thick gloom of darkest night. 'What place is this?' asked Scrooge.

'A place where miners live, who labour in the bowels of the earth,' returned the Spirit. 'But they know me. See!'

A light shone from the window of a hut, and swiftly they

advanced towards it. Passing through the wall of mud and stone, they found a cheerful company assembled round a glowing fire. An old, old man and woman, with their children and their children's children, and another generation beyond that, all decked out gaily in their holiday attire. The old man, in a voice that seldom rose above the howling of the wind upon the barren waste, was singing them a Christmas song; it had been a very old song when he was a boy; and from time to time they all joined in the chorus. So surely as they raised their voices, the old man got quite blithe and loud; and so surely as they stopped, his vigour sank again.

The Spirit did not tarry here, but bade Scrooge hold his robe, and, passing on above the moor, sped whither? Not to sea? To sea. To Scrooge's horror, looking back, he saw the last of the land, a frightful range of rocks, behind them; and his ears were deafened by the thundering of water, as it rolled and roared, and raged among the dreadful caverns it had worn, and fiercely tried to undermine the earth.

Built upon a dismal reef of sunken rocks, some league or so from shore, on which the waters chafed and dashed, the wild year through, there stood a solitary lighthouse. Great heaps of seaweed clung to its base, and storm-birds—born of the wind, one might suppose, as seaweed of the water—rose and fell about it, like the waves they skimmed.

But, even here, two men who watched the light had made a fire, that through the loophole in the thick stone wall shed out a ray of brightness on the awful sea. Joining their horny hands over the rough table at which they sat, they wished each other Merry Christmas in their can of grog; and one of them—the elder too, with his face all damaged and scarred with hard weather, as the figure-head of an old ship might be —struck up a sturdy song that was like a gale in itself.

Again the Ghost sped on, above the black and heaving sea—on, on—until being far away, as he told Scrooge, from any shore, they lighted on a ship. They stood beside the helmsman at the wheel, the look-out in the bow, the officers who had the watch; dark, ghostly figures in their several stations; but every man among them hummed a Christmas tune, or had a Christmas thought, or spoke below his breath to his companion of some bygone Christmas Day, with homeward hopes belonging to it. And every man on board, waking or sleeping, good or bad, had had a kinder word for one another on that day than on any day in the year; and had shared to some extent in its festivities; and had remembered those he cared for at a distance, and had known that they delighted to remember him.

It was a great surprise to Scrooge, while listening to the moaning of the wind, and thinking what a solemn thing it was to move on through the lonely darkness over an unknown abyss, whose depths were secrets as profound as death: it was a great surprise to Scrooge, while thus engaged, to hear a hearty laugh. It was a much greater surprise to Scrooge to recognise it as his own nephew's and to find himself in a bright, dry, gleaming room, with the Spirit standing smiling by his side, and looking at that same nephew with approving affability!

'Ha, ha!' laughed Scrooge's nephew. 'Ha, ha, ha!'

If you should happen, by any unlikely chance, to know a man more blessed in a laugh than Scrooge's nephew, all I can say is, I should like to know him too. Introduce him to me, and I'll cultivate his acquaintance. It is a fair, even-handed, noble adjustment of things, that while there is infection in disease and sorrow, there is nothing in the world so irresistibly contagious as laughter and good-humour. When

Scrooge's nephew laughed in this way—holding his sides, rolling his head, and twisting his face into the most extravagant contortions—Scrooge's niece, by marriage, laughed as heartily as he. And their assembled friends, being not a bit behindhand, roared out lustily.

'Ha, ha! Ha, ha, ha, ha!'

'He said that Christmas was a humbug, as I live!' cried Scrooge's nephew. 'He believed it, too!'

'More shame for him, Fred!' said Scrooge's niece indignantly. Bless those women! they never do anything by halves. They are always in earnest.

She was very pretty; exceedingly pretty. With a dimpled, surprised-looking, capital face; a ripe little mouth, that seemed made to be kissed—as no doubt it was; all kinds of good little dots about her chin, that melted into one another when she laughed; and the sunniest pair of eyes you ever saw in any little creature's head. Altogether she was what you would have called provoking, you know; but satisfactory, too. Oh, perfectly satisfactory!

'He's a comical old fellow,' said Scrooge's nephew, 'that's the truth; and not so pleasant as he might be. However, his offences carry their own punishment, and I have nothing to say against him.'

'I'm sure he is very rich, Fred,' hinted Scrooge's niece. 'At least, you always tell *me* so.'

'What of that, my dear?' said Scrooge's nephew. 'His wealth is of no use to him. He don't do any good with it. He don't make himself comfortable with it. He hasn't the satisfaction of thinking—ha, ha, ha!—that he is ever going to benefit Us with it.'

'I have no patience with him,' observed Scrooge's niece.

Scrooge's niece's sisters, and all the other ladies, expressed the same opinion.

'Oh, I have!' said Scrooge's nephew. 'I am sorry for him; I couldn't be angry with him if I tried. Who suffers by his ill whims? Himself always. Here he takes it into his head to dislike us, and he won't come and dine with us. What's the consequence? He don't lose much of a dinner.'

'Indeed, I think he loses a very good dinner,' interrupted Scrooge's niece. Everybody else said the same, and they must be allowed to have been competent judges, because they had just had dinner; and with the dessert upon the table, were clustered round the fire, by lamplight.

'Well! I am very glad to hear it,' said Scrooge's nephew, 'because I haven't any great faith in these young housekeep-ers. What do *you* say, Topper?'

Topper had clearly got his eye upon one of Scrooge's niece's sisters, for he answered that a bachelor was a wretched outcast, who had no right to express an opinion on the subject. Whereat Scrooge's niece's sister—the plump one with the lace tucker: not the one with the roses—blushed.

'Do go on, Fred,' said Scrooge's niece, clapping her hands. 'He never finishes what he begins to say! He is such a ridicu-lous fellow!'

Scrooge's nephew revelled in another laugh, and as it was impossible to keep the infection off, though the plump sister tried hard to do it with aromatic vinegar, his example was unanimously followed.

'I was only going to say,' said Scrooge's nephew, 'that the consequence of his taking a dislike to us, and not making merry with us, is, as I think, that he loses some pleasant moments, which could do him no harm. I am sure he loses pleasanter companions than he can find in his own thoughts, either in his mouldy old office or his dusty chambers. I mean to give him the same chance every year, whether he likes it or not, for I pity him. He may rail at Christmas till he dies, but he can't help thinking better of it—I defy him—if he finds me going there, in good temper, year after year, and saying, "Uncle Scrooge, how are you?" If it only put him in the vein to leave his poor clerk fifty pounds, *that's* something; and I think I shook him yesterday.'

It was their turn to laugh now, at the notion of his shaking Scrooge. But being thoroughly good-natured, and not much caring what they laughed at, so that they laughed at any rate, he encouraged them in their merriment, and passed the bottle, joyously.

After tea they had some music. For they were a musical family, and knew what they were about when they sung a Glee or Catch, I can assure you: especially Topper, who could growl away in the bass like a good one, and never swell the large veins in his forehead, or get red in the face over it. Scrooge's niece played well upon the harp; and played, among other tunes, a simple little air (a mere nothing: you might learn to whistle it in two minutes) which had been familiar to the child who fetched Scrooge from the boarding-school, as he had been reminded by the Ghost of Christmas Past. When this strain of music sounded, all the things that Ghost had shown him came upon his mind; he softened more and more; and thought that if he could have listened to it often, years ago, he might have cultivated the kindnesses of life for his own happiness with his own hands, without resorting to the sexton's spade that buried Jacob Marley.

But they didn't devote the whole evening to music. After a while they played at forfeits; for it is good to be children sometimes, and never better than at Christmas, when its mighty Founder was a child himself. Stop! There was first a game at blind man's-buff. Of course there was. And I no more believe Topper was really blind than I believe he had eyes in his boots. My opinion is, that it was a done thing between him and Scrooge's nephew; and that the Ghost of Christmas Present knew it. The way he went after that plump sister in the lace tucker was an outrage on the credulity of human nature. Knocking down the fire-irons, tumbling over the chairs, bumping up against the piano, smothering himself amongst the curtains, wherever she went, there went he! He always knew where the plump sister was. He wouldn't catch anybody else. If you had fallen up against him (as some of them did) on purpose, he would have made a feint of endeavouring to seize you, which would have been an affront to your understanding, and would instantly have sidled off in the direction of the plump sister. She often cried out that it wasn't fair; and it really was not. But when, at last, he caught her; when, in spite of all her silken rustlings, and her rapid flutterings past him, he got her into a corner whence there was no escape; then his conduct was the most execrable. For his pretending not to know her; his pretending that it was necessary to touch her head-dress, and further to assure himself of her identity by pressing a certain ring upon her finger, and a certain chain about her neck; was vile, monstrous! No doubt she told him her opinion of it when, another blind man being in office, they were so very confidential together behind the curtains.

Scrooge's niece was not one of the blind man's-buff party, but was made comfortable with a large chair and a footstool, in a snug corner where the Ghost and Scrooge were close behind her. But she joined in the forfeits, and loved her love to admiration with all the letters of the alphabet. Likewise at the game of How, When, and Where, she was very great, and, to the secret joy of Scrooge's nephew, beat her sisters hollow; though they were sharp girls too, as Topper could have told you. There might have been twenty people there, young and old, but they all played, and so did Scrooge; for wholly forgetting, in the interest he had in what was going on, that his voice made no sound in their ears, he sometimes came out with his guess quite loud, and very often guessed right, too; for the sharpest needle, best Whitechapel, warranted not to cut in the eye, was not sharper than Scrooge, blunt as he took it in his head to be.

The Ghost was greatly pleased to find him in this mood, and looked upon him with such favour that he begged like a boy to be allowed to stay until the guests departed. But this the Spirit said could not be done.

'Here is a new game,' said Scrooge. 'One half-hour, Spirit, only one!'

It was a game called Yes and No, where Scrooge's nephew had to think of something, and the rest must find out what, he only answering to their questions yes or no, as the case was. The brisk fire of questioning to which he was exposed elicited from him that he was thinking of an animal, a live animal, rather a disagreeable animal, a savage animal, an animal that growled and grunted sometimes, and talked sometimes and lived in London, and walked about the streets, and wasn't made a show of, and wasn't led by anybody, and didn't live in a menagerie, and was never killed in a market, and was not a horse, or an ass, or a cow, or a bull, or a tiger, or a dog, or a pig, or a cat, or a bear. At every fresh question that was put to him, this nephew burst into a fresh roar of laughter; and was so inexpressibly tickled, that he was obliged to get up off the sofa and stamp. At last the plump sister, falling into a similar state, cried out:

'I have found it out! I know what it is, Fred! I know what it is!'

'What is it?' cried Fred.

'It's your uncle Scro-o-o-o-oge.'

Which it certainly was. Admiration was the universal sentiment, though some objected that the reply to 'Is it a bear?' ought to have been 'Yes'; inasmuch as an answer in the negative was sufficient to have diverted their thoughts from Mr. Scrooge, supposing they had ever had any tendency that way.

'He has given us plenty of merriment, I am sure,' said Fred, 'and it would be ungrateful not to drink his health. Here is a glass of mulled wine ready to our hand at the moment; and I say, "Uncle Scrooge!"'

'Well! Uncle Scrooge!' they cried.

'A merry Christmas and a happy New Year to the old man, whatever he is!' said Scrooge's nephew. 'He wouldn't take it from me, but may he have it, nevertheless. Uncle Scrooge!'

Uncle Scrooge had imperceptibly become so gay and light of heart, that he would have pledged the unconscious company in return, and thanked them in an inaudible speech, if the Ghost had given him time. But the whole scene passed off in the breath of the last word spoken by his nephew; and he and the Spirit were again upon their travels.

Much they saw, and far they went, and many homes they visited, but always with a happy end. The Spirit stood beside sick-beds, and they were cheerful; on foreign lands, and they were close at home; by struggling men, and they were patient in their greater hope; by poverty, and it was rich. In almshouse, hospital, and gaol, in misery's every refuge, where vain man in his little brief authority had not made fast the door, and barred the Spirit out, he left his blessing and taught Scrooge his precepts.

It was a long night, if it were only a night; but Scrooge had his doubts of this, because the Christmas holidays appeared to be condensed into the space of time they passed together. It was strange, too, that, while Scrooge remained unaltered in his outward form, the Ghost grew older, clearly older. Scrooge had observed this change, but never spoke of it until they left a children's Twelfth-Night party, when, looking at the Spirit as they stood together in an open place, he noticed that its hair was grey.

'Are spirits' lives so short?' asked Scrooge.

'My life upon this globe is very brief,' replied the Ghost. 'It ends to-night.'

'To-night!' cried Scrooge.

'To-night at midnight. Hark! The time is drawing near.'

The chimes were ringing the three-quarters past eleven at that moment.

'Forgive me if I am not justified in what I ask,' said Scrooge, looking intently at the Spirit's robe, 'but I see something strange, and not belonging to yourself, protruding from your skirts. Is it a foot or a claw?'

'It might be a claw, for the flesh there is upon it,' was the Spirit's sorrowful reply. 'Look here!'

From the foldings of its robe it brought two children, wretched, abject, frightful, hideous, miserable. They knelt down at its feet, and clung upon the outside of its garment.

'O Man! look here! Look, look down here!' exclaimed the Ghost.

They were a boy and girl. Yellow, meagre, ragged, scowling, wolfish, but prostrate, too, in their humility. Where graceful youth should have filled their features out, and touched them with its freshest tints, a stale and shrivelled hand, like that of age, had pinched and twisted them, and pulled them into shreds. Where angels might have sat enthroned, devils lurked, and glared out menacing. No change, no degradation, no perversion of humanity in any grade, through all the mysteries of wonderful creation, has monsters half so horrible and dread.

Scrooge started back, appalled. Having them shown to him in this way, he tried to say they were fine children, but the words choked themselves, rather than be parties to a lie of such enormous magnitude.

'Spirit! are they yours?' Scrooge could say no more.

'They are Man's,' said the Spirit, looking down upon them. 'And they cling to me, appealing from their fathers. This boy is Ignorance. This girl is Want. Beware of them both, and all of their degree, but most of all beware this boy, for on his brow I see that written which is Doom, unless the writing be erased. Deny it!' cried the Spirit, stretching out his hand towards the city. 'Slander those who tell it ye! Admit it for your factious purposes, and make it worse! And bide the end!'

'Have they no refuge or resource?' cried Scrooge.

'Are there no prisons?' said the Spirit, turning on him for the last time with his own words. 'Are there no workhouses?'

The bell struck Twelve.

Scrooge looked about him for the Ghost, and saw it not. As the last stroke ceased to vibrate, he remembered the prediction of old Jacob Marley, and, lifting up his eyes, beheld a solemn Phantom, draped and hooded, coming like a mist along the ground towards him.

STAVE FOUR

## The Last of the Spirits

THE PHANTOM SLOWLY, GRAVELY, SILENTLY
approached. When it came near him, Scrooge bent down
upon his knee; for in the very air through which this Spirit
moved it seemed to scatter gloom and mystery.

It was shrouded in a deep black garment, which concealed
its head, its face, its form, and left nothing of it visible, save
one outstretched hand. But for this, it would have been diffi-
cult to detach its figure from the night, and separate it from
the darkness by which it was surrounded.

He felt that it was tall and stately when it came beside
him, and that its mysterious presence filled him with a
solemn dread. He knew no more, for the Spirit neither spoke
nor moved.

'I am in the presence of the Ghost of Christmas Yet to
Come?' said Scrooge.

The Spirit answered not, but pointed onward with its
hand.

'You are about to show me shadows of the things that have not happened, but will happen in the time before us,' Scrooge pursued. 'Is that so, Spirit?'

The upper portion of the garment was contracted for an instant in its folds, as if the Spirit had inclined its head. That was the only answer he received.

Although well used to ghostly company by this time, Scrooge feared the silent shape so much that his legs trembled beneath him, and he found that he could hardly stand when he prepared to follow it. The Spirit paused a moment, as observing his condition, and giving him time to recover.

But Scrooge was all the worse for this. It thrilled him with a vague, uncertain horror to know that, behind the dusky shroud, there were ghostly eyes intently fixed upon him, while he, though he stretched his own to the utmost, could see nothing but a spectral hand and one great heap of black.

'Ghost of the Future!' he exclaimed, 'I fear you more than any spectre I have seen. But as I know your purpose is to do me good, and as I hope to live to be another man from what I was, I am prepared to bear your company, and do it with a thankful heart. Will you not speak to me?'

It gave him no reply. The hand was pointed straight before them.

'Lead on!' said Scrooge. 'Lead on! The night is waning fast, and it is precious time to me, I know. Lead on, Spirit!'

The Phantom moved away as it had come towards him. Scrooge followed in the shadow of its dress, which bore him up, he thought, and carried him along.

They scarcely seemed to enter the City; for the City rather seemed to spring up about them, and encompass them of its own act. But there they were in the heart of it; on 'Change, amongst the merchants, who hurried up and down, and chinked the money in their pockets, and conversed in groups, and looked at their watches, and trifled thoughtfully with their great gold seals, and so forth, as Scrooge had seen them often.

The Spirit stopped beside one little knot of business men. Observing that the hand was pointed to them, Scrooge advanced to listen to their talk.

'No,' said a great fat man with a monstrous chin, 'I don't know much about it either way. I only know he's dead.'

'When did he die?' inquired another.

'Last night, I believe.'

'Why, what was the matter with him?' asked a third, taking a vast quantity of snuff out of a very large snuff-box. 'I thought he'd never die.'

'God knows,' said the first, with a yawn.

'What has he done with his money?' asked a red-faced gentleman with a pendulous excrescence on the end of his nose, that shook like the gills of a turkey-cock.

'I haven't heard,' said the man with the large chin, yawning again. 'Left it to his company, perhaps. He hasn't left it to *me*. That's all I know.'

This pleasantry was received with a general laugh.

'It's likely to be a very cheap funeral,' said the same speaker; 'for, upon my life, I don't know of anybody to go to it. Suppose we make up a party, and volunteer?'

'I don't mind going if a lunch is provided,' observed the gentleman with the excrescence on his nose. 'But I must be fed if I make one.'

Another laugh.

'Well, I am the most disinterested among you, after all,' said the first speaker, 'for I never wear black gloves, and I never eat lunch. But I'll offer to go if anybody else will. When

I come to think of it, I'm not at all sure that I wasn't his most particular friend; for we used to stop and speak whenever we met. Bye, bye!'

Speakers and listeners strolled away, and mixed with other groups. Scrooge knew the men, and looked towards the Spirit for an explanation.

The phantom glided on into a street. Its finger pointed to two persons meeting. Scrooge listened again, thinking that the explanation might lie here.

He knew these men, also, perfectly. They were men of business: very wealthy, and of great importance. He had made a point always of standing well in their esteem in a business point of view, that is; strictly in a business point of view.

'How are you?' said one.

'How are you?' returned the other.

'Well!' said the first, 'old Scratch has got his own at last, hey?'

'So I am told,' returned the second. 'Cold, isn't it?'

'Seasonable for Christmas-time. You are not a skater, I suppose?'

'No, no. Something else to think of. Good-morning!'

Not another word. That was their meeting, their conversation, and their parting.

Scrooge was at first inclined to be surprised that the Spirit should attach importance to conversations apparently so trivial; but feeling assured that they must have some hidden purpose, he set himself to consider what it was likely to be. They could scarcely be supposed to have any bearing on the death of Jacob, his old partner, for that was Past, and this Ghost's province was the Future. Nor could he think of any one immediately connected with himself to whom he could apply them. But nothing doubting that, to whomsoever they applied, they had some latent moral for his own improvement, he resolved to treasure up every word he heard, and everything he saw; and especially to observe the shadow of himself when it appeared. For he had an expectation that the conduct of his future self would give him the clue he missed, and would render the solution of these riddles easy.

He looked about in that very place for his own image, but another man stood in his accustomed corner; and though the clock pointed to his usual time of day for being there, he saw no likeness of himself among the multitudes that poured in through the Porch. It gave him little surprise, however; for he had been revolving in his mind a change of life, and thought and hoped he saw his new-born resolutions carried out in this.

Quiet and dark, beside him stood the Phantom, with its outstretched hand. When he roused himself from his thoughtful quest, he fancied, from the turn of the hand, and its situation in reference to himself, that the Unseen Eyes were looking at him keenly. It made him shudder, and feel very cold.

They left the busy scene, and went into an obscure part of the town, where Scrooge had never penetrated before, although he recognised its situation and its bad repute. The ways were foul and narrow; the shop and houses wretched; the people half naked, drunken, slipshod, ugly. Alleys and archways, like so many cesspools, disgorged their offences of smell and dirt, and life upon the straggling streets; and the whole quarter reeked with crime, with filth, and misery.

Far in this den of infamous resort, there was a low-browed, beetling shop, below a penthouse roof, where iron, old rags, bottles, bones, and greasy offal were bought. Upon the floor within were piled up heaps of rusty keys, nails, chains, hinges, files, scales, weights, and refuse iron of all kinds. Secrets that few would like to scrutinise were bred and hidden in mountains of unseemly rags, masses of corrupted fat, and sepulchres of bones. Sitting in among the wares he dealt in, by a charcoal stove made of old bricks, was a grey-haired rascal, nearly seventy years of age, who had screened himself from the cold air without by a frouzy curtaining of miscellaneous tatters hung upon a line and smoked his pipe in all the luxury of calm retirement.

Scrooge and the Phantom came into the presence of this man, just as a woman with a heavy bundle slunk into the shop. But she had scarcely entered, when another woman, similarly laden, came in too; and she was closely followed by a man in faded black, who was no less startled by the sight of them than they had been upon the recognition of each other. After a short period of blank astonishment, in which the old man with the pipe had joined them, they all three burst into a laugh.

'Let the charwoman alone to be the first!' cried she who had entered first. 'Let the laundress alone to be the second; and let the undertaker's man alone to be the third. Look here, old Joe, here's a chance! If we haven't all three met here without meaning it!'

'You couldn't have met in a better place,' said old Joe, removing his pipe from his mouth. 'Come into the parlour. You were made free of it long ago, you know; and the other two an't strangers. Stop till I shut the door of the shop. Ah! how it skreeks! There an't such a rusty bit of metal in the place as its own hinges, I believe; and I'm sure there's no such old bones here as mine. Ha! ha! We're all suitable to our calling, we're well matched. Come into the parlour. Come into the parlour.'

The parlour was the space behind the screen of rags. The old man raked the fire together with an old stair-rod, and having trimmed his smoky lamp (for it was night) with the stem of his pipe, put it into his mouth again.

While he did this, the woman who had already spoken threw her bundle on the floor, and sat down in a flaunting manner on a stool, crossing her elbows on her knees, and looking with a bold defiance at the other two.

'What odds, then? What odds, Mrs. Dilber?' said the woman. 'Every person has a right to take care of themselves. *He* always did!'

'That's true, indeed!' said the laundress. 'No man more so.'

'Why, then, don't stand staring as if you was afraid, woman! Who's the wiser? We're not going to pick holes in each other's coats, I suppose?'

'No, indeed!' said Mrs. Dilber and the man together. 'We should hope not.'

'Very well then!' cried the woman. 'That's enough. Who's the worse for the loss of a few things like these? Not a dead man, I suppose?'

'No, indeed,' said Mrs. Dilber, laughing.

'If he wanted to keep 'em after he was dead, a wicked old screw,' pursued the woman, 'why wasn't he natural in his lifetime? If he had been, he'd have had somebody to look after him when he was struck with Death, instead of lying gasping out his last there, alone by himself.'

'It's the truest word that ever was spoke,' said Mrs. Dilber. 'It's a judgment on him.'

'I wish it was a little heavier judgment,' replied the woman: 'and it should have been, you may depend upon it, if I could have laid my hands on anything else. Open that bundle, old Joe, and let me know the value of it. Speak out plain. I'm not afraid to be the first, nor afraid for them to see it. We knew pretty well that we were helping ourselves before we met here, I believe. It's no sin. Open the bundle, Joe.'

But the gallantry of her friends would not allow of this; and the man in faded black, mounting the breach first, produced *his* plunder. It was not extensive. A seal or two, a pencil-case, a pair of sleeve-buttons, and a brooch of no great value, were all. They were severally examined and appraised by old Joe, who chalked the sums he was disposed to give for each upon the wall, and added them up into a total when he found that there was nothing more to come.

'That's your account,' said Joe, 'and I wouldn't give another sixpence, if I was to be boiled for not doing it. Who's next?'

Mrs. Dilber was next. Sheets and towels, a little wearing apparel, two old fashioned silver teaspoons, a pair of sugar-tongs, and a few boots. Her account was stated on the wall in the same manner.

'I always give too much to ladies. It's a weakness of mine, and that's the way I ruin myself,' said old Joe. 'That's your account. If you asked me for another penny, and made it an open question, I'd repent of being so liberal, and knock off half-a-crown.'

'And now undo *my* bundle, Joe,' said the first woman.

Joe went down on his knees for the greater convenience of opening it, and, having unfastened a great many knots, dragged out a large heavy roll of some dark stuff.

'What do you call this?' said Joe. 'Bed-curtains?'

'Ah!' returned the woman, laughing and leaning forward on her crossed arms. 'Bed-curtains!'

'You don't mean to say you took 'em down, rings and all, with him lying there?' said Joe.

'Yes, I do,' replied the woman. 'Why not?'

'You were born to make your fortune,' said Joe, 'and you'll certainly do it.'

'I certainly shan't hold my hand, when I can get anything in it by reaching it out, for the sake of such a man as he was, I promise you, Joe,' returned the woman coolly. 'Don't drop that oil upon the blankets, now.'

'His blankets?' asked Joe.

'Whose else's do you think?' replied the woman. 'He isn't likely to take cold without 'em, I dare say.'

'I hope he didn't die of anything catching? Eh?' said old Joe, stopping in his work, and looking up.

'Don't you be afraid of that,' returned the woman. 'I an't so fond of his company that I'd loiter about him for such things, if he did. Ah! you may look through that shirt till your eyes ache, but you won't find a hole in it, nor a threadbare place. It's the best he had, and a fine one too. They'd have wasted it, if it hadn't been for me.'

'What do you call wasting of it?' asked old Joe.

'Putting it on him to be buried in, to be sure,' replied the woman, with a laugh. 'Somebody was fool enough to do it, but I took it off again. If calico an't good enough for such a purpose, it isn't good enough for anything. It's quite as becoming to the body. He can't look uglier than he did in that one.'

Scrooge listened to this dialogue in horror. As they sat grouped about their spoil, in the scanty light afforded by the old man's lamp, he viewed them with a detestation and disgust which could hardly have been greater, though they had been obscene demons marketing the corpse itself.

'Ha, ha!' laughed the same woman when old Joe producing a flannel bag with money in it, told out their several gains upon the ground. 'This is the end of it, you see! He frightened every one away from him when he was alive, to profit us when he was dead! Ha, ha, ha!'

'Spirit!' said Scrooge, shuddering from head to foot. 'I see, I see. The case of this unhappy man might be my own. My life tends that way now. Merciful heaven, what is this?'

He recoiled in terror, for the scene had changed, and now he almost touched a bed—a bare, uncurtained bed—on which, beneath a ragged sheet, there lay a something covered up, which, though it was dumb, announced itself in awful language.

The room was very dark, too dark to be observed with any accuracy, though Scrooge glanced round it in obedience to a secret impulse, anxious to know what kind of room it was. A pale light, rising in the outer air, fell straight upon the bed; and on it, plundered and bereft, unwatched, unwept, uncared for, was the body of this man.

Scrooge glanced towards the Phantom. Its steady hand was pointed to the head. The cover was so carelessly adjusted that the slightest raising of it, the motion of a finger upon Scrooge's part, would have disclosed the face. He thought of it, felt how easy it would be to do, and longed to do it; but he had no more power to withdraw the veil than to dismiss the spectre at his side.

Oh, cold, cold, rigid, dreadful Death, set up thine altar here, and dress it with such terrors as thou hast at thy command; for this is thy dominion! But of the loved, revered, and honoured head thou canst not turn one hair to thy dread purposes, or make one feature odious. It is not that the hand is heavy, and will fall down when released; it is not that the heart and pulse are still; but that the hand was open, generous, and true; the heart brave, warm, and tender, and the pulse a man's. Strike, Shadow, strike! And see his good deeds springing from the wound, to sow the world with life immortal!

No voice pronounced these words in Scrooge's ears, and yet he heard them when he looked upon the bed. He thought, if this man could be raised up now, what would be his foremost thoughts? Avarice, hard dealing, griping cares? They have brought him to a rich end, truly!

He lay in the dark, empty house, with not a man, a woman, or a child to say he was kind to me in this or that, and for the memory of one kind word I will be kind to him. A cat was tearing at the door, and there was a sound of gnawing rats beneath the hearthstone. What *they* wanted in the room of death, and why they were so restless and disturbed, Scrooge did not dare to think.

'Spirit!' he said, 'this is a fearful place. In leaving it, I shall not leave its lesson, trust me. Let us go!'

Still the Ghost pointed with an unmoved finger to the head.

'I understand you,' Scrooge returned, 'and I would do it if I could. But I have not the power, Spirit. I have not the power.'

Again it seemed to look upon him.

'If there is any person in the town who feels emotion caused by this man's death,' said Scrooge, quite agonised, 'show that person to me, Spirit, I beseech you!'

The Phantom spread its dark robe before him for a

moment, like a wing; and, withdrawing it, revealed a room by daylight, where a mother and her children were.

She was expecting some one, and with anxious eagerness; for she walked up and down the room, started at every sound, looked out from the window, glanced at the clock, tried, but in vain, to work with her needle, and could hardly bear the voices of her children in their play.

At length the long-expected knock was heard. She hurried to the door, and met her husband; a man whose face was careworn and depressed, though he was young. There was a remarkable expression in it now, a kind of serious delight of which he felt ashamed, and which he struggled to repress.

He sat down to the dinner that had been hoarding for him by the fire, and when she asked him faintly what news (which was not until after a long silence), he appeared embarrassed how to answer.

'Is it good,' she said, 'or bad?' to help him.

'Bad,' he answered.

'We are quite ruined?'

'No. There is hope yet, Caroline.'

'If *he* relents,' she said, amazed, 'there is! Nothing is past hope, if such a miracle has happened.'

'He is past relenting,' said her husband. 'He is dead.'

She was a mild and patient creature, if her face spoke truth; but she was thankful in her soul to hear it, and she said so with clasped hands. She prayed forgiveness the next moment, and was sorry; but the first was the emotion of her heart.

'What the half-drunken woman, whom I told you of last night, said to me when I tried to see him and obtain a week's delay—and what I thought was a mere excuse to avoid me—

turns out to have been quite true. He was not only very ill, but dying, then.'

'To whom will our debt be transferred?'

'I don't know. But, before that time, we shall be ready with the money; and even though we were not, it would be bad fortune indeed to find so merciless a creditor in his successor. We may sleep to-night with light hearts, Caroline!'

Yes. Soften it as they would, their hearts were lighter. The children's faces, hushed and clustered round to hear what they so little understood, were brighter; and it was a happier house for this man's death! The only emotion that the Ghost could show him, caused by the event, was one of pleasure.

'Let me see some tenderness connected with a death,' said Scrooge; 'or that dark chamber, Spirit, which we left just now, will be for ever present to me.'

The Ghost conducted him through several streets familiar to his feet; and as they went along, Scrooge looked here and there to find himself, but nowhere was he to be seen. They entered poor Bob Cratchit's house; the dwelling he had visited before; and found the mother and the children seated round the fire.

Quiet. Very quiet. The noisy little Cratchits were as still as statues in one corner, and sat looking up at Peter, who had a book before him. The mother and her daughters were engaged in sewing. But surely they were very quiet!

'"And he took a child, and set him in the midst of them."'

Where had Scrooge heard those words? He had not dreamed them. The boy must have read them out as he and the Spirit crossed the threshold. Why did he not go on?

The mother laid her work upon the table, and put her hand up to her face.

'The colour hurts my eyes,' she said.

The colour? Ah, poor Tiny Tim!

'They're better now again,' said Cratchit's wife. 'It makes them weak by candle-light; and I wouldn't show weak eyes to your father when he comes home for the world. It must be near his time.'

'Past it rather,' Peter answered, shutting up his book. 'But I think he has walked a little slower than he used, these few last evenings, mother.'

They were very quiet again. At last she said, and in a steady, cheerful voice, that only faltered once:

'I have known him walk with—I have known him walk with Tiny Tim upon his shoulder very fast indeed.'

'And so have I,' cried Peter. 'Often.'

'And so have I,' exclaimed another. So had all.

'But he was very light to carry,' she resumed, intent upon her work, 'and his father loved him so, that it was no trouble, no trouble. And there is your father at the door!'

She hurried out to meet him; and little Bob in his comforter—he had need of it, poor fellow—came in. His tea was ready for him on the hob, and they all tried who should help him to it most. Then the two young Cratchits got upon his knees, and laid, each child, a little cheek against his face, as if they said, 'Don't mind it, father. Don't be grieved!'

Bob was very cheerful with them, and spoke pleasantly to all the family. He looked at the work upon the table, and praised the industry and speed of Mrs. Cratchit and the girls. They would be done long before Sunday, he said.

'Sunday! You went to-day, then, Robert?' said his wife.

'Yes, my dear,' returned Bob. 'I wish you could have gone. It would have done you good to see how green a place it is. But you'll see it often. I promised him that I would walk there on a Sunday. My little, little child!' cried Bob. 'My little child!'

He broke down all at once. He couldn't help it. If he could have helped it, he and his child would have been farther apart, perhaps, than they were.

He left the room, and went upstairs into the room above, which was lighted cheerfully, and hung with Christmas. There was a chair set close beside the child, and there were signs of some one having been there lately. Poor Bob sat down in it, and when he had thought a little and composed himself, he kissed the little face. He was reconciled to what had happened, and went down again quite happy.

They drew about the fire, and talked, the girls and mother working still. Bob told them of the extraordinary kindness of Mr. Scrooge's nephew, whom he had scarcely seen but once, and who, meeting him in the street that day, and seeing that he looked a little—'just a little down, you know,' said Bob, inquired what had happened to distress him. 'On which,' said Bob, 'for he is the pleasantest-spoken gentleman you ever heard, I told him. "I am heartily sorry for it, Mr. Cratchit," he said, "and heartily sorry for your good wife." By-the-bye, how he ever knew *that* I don't know.'

'Knew what, my dear?'

'Why, that you were a good wife,' replied Bob.

'Everybody knows that,' said Peter.

'Very well observed, my boy!' cried Bob. 'I hope they do. "Heartily sorry," he said, "for your good wife. If I can be of service to you in any way," he said, giving me his card, "that's where I live. Pray come to me." Now, it wasn't,' cried Bob, 'for the sake of anything he might be able to do for us, so much as for his kind way, that this was quite delightful. It really seemed as if he had known our Tiny Tim, and felt with us.'

'I'm sure he's a good soul!' said Mrs. Cratchit.

'You would be sure of it, my dear,' returned Bob, 'if you saw and spoke to him. I shouldn't be at all surprised—mark what I say!—if he got Peter a better situation.'

'Only hear that, Peter,' said Mrs. Cratchit.

'And then,' cried one of the girls, 'Peter will be keeping company with some one, and setting up for himself.'

'Get along with you!' retorted Peter, grinning.

'It's just as likely as not,' said Bob, 'one of these days; though there's plenty of time for that, my dear. But, however and whenever we part from one another, I am sure we shall none of us forget poor Tiny Tim—shall we—or this first parting that there was among us?'

'Never, father!' cried they all.

'And I know,' said Bob, 'I know, my dears, that when we recollect how patient and how mild he was; although he was a little, little child; we shall not quarrel easily among ourselves, and forget poor Tiny Tim in doing it.'

'No, never, father!' they all cried again.

'I am very happy,' said little Bob, 'I am very happy!'

Mrs. Cratchit kissed him, his daughters kissed him, the two young Cratchits kissed him, and Peter and himself shook hands. Spirit of Tiny Tim, thy childish essence was from God!

'Spectre,' said Scrooge, 'something informs me that our parting moment is at hand. I know it but I know not how. Tell me what man that was whom we saw lying dead?'

The Ghost of Christmas Yet to Come conveyed him, as before—though at a different time, he thought: indeed there seemed no order in these latter visions, save that they were in the Future—into the resorts of business men, but showed him not himself. Indeed, the Spirit did not stay for anything, but went straight on, as to the end just now desired, until besought by Scrooge to tarry for a moment.

'This court,' said Scrooge, 'through which we hurry now, is where my place of occupation is, and has been for a length of time. I see the house. Let me behold what I shall be in days to come.'

The Spirit stopped; the hand was pointed elsewhere.

'The house is yonder,' Scrooge exclaimed. 'Why do you point away?'

The inexorable finger underwent no change.

Scrooge hastened to the window of his office, and looked in. It was an office still, but not his. The furniture was not the same, and the figure in the chair was not himself. The Phantom pointed as before.

He joined it once again, and, wondering why and whither he had gone, accompanied it until they reached an iron gate. He paused to look round before entering.

A churchyard. Here, then, the wretched man, whose name he had now to learn, lay underneath the ground. It was a worthy place. Walled in by houses; overrun by grass and weeds, the growth of vegetation's death, not life; choked up with too much burying; fat with repleted appetite. A worthy place!

The Spirit stood among the graves, and pointed down to One. He advanced towards it trembling. The Phantom was exactly as it had been, but he dreaded that he saw new meaning in its solemn shape.

'Before I draw nearer to that stone to which you point,' said Scrooge, 'answer me one question. Are these the shadows of the things that Will be, or are they shadows of the things that May be only?'

Still the Ghost pointed downward to the grave by which it stood.

'Men's courses will foreshadow certain ends, to which, if persevered in, they must lead,' said Scrooge. 'But if the courses be departed from, the ends will change. Say it is thus with what you show me!'

The Spirit was immovable as ever.

Scrooge crept towards it, trembling as he went; and, following the finger, read upon the stone of the neglected grave his own name, EBENEZER SCROOGE.

'Am I that man who lay upon the bed?' he cried upon his knees.

The finger pointed from the grave to him, and back again.

'No, Spirit! Oh no, no!'

The finger still was there.

'Spirit!' he cried, tight clutching at its robe, 'hear me! I am not the man I was. I will not be the man I must have been but for this intercourse. Why show me this, if I am past all hope?'

For the first time the hand appeared to shake.

'Good Spirit,' he pursued, as down upon the ground he fell before it, 'your nature intercedes for me, and pities me. Assure me that I yet may change these shadows you have shown me by an altered life?'

The kind hand trembled.

'I will honour Christmas in my heart, and try to keep it all the year. I will live in the Past, the Present, and the Future. The Spirits of all Three shall strive within me. I will not shut out the lessons that they teach. Oh, tell me I may sponge away the writing on this stone!'

In his agony he caught the spectral hand. It sought to free itself, but he was strong in his entreaty, and detained it. The Spirit stronger yet, repulsed him.

Holding up his hands in a last prayer to have his fate reversed, he saw an alteration in the Phantom's hood and dress. It shrunk, collapsed, and dwindled down into a bedpost.

# STAVE FIVE

## The End of It

YES! AND THE BEDPOST WAS HIS OWN. THE BED WAS his own, the room was his own. Best and happiest of all, the Time before him was his own, to make amends in!

'I will live in the Past, the Present, and the Future!' Scrooge repeated as he scrambled out of bed. 'The Spirits of all Three shall strive within me. O Jacob Marley! Heaven and the Christmas Time be praised for this! I say it on my knees, old Jacob; on my knees!'

He was so fluttered and so glowing with his good intentions, that his broken voice would scarcely answer to his call. He had been sobbing violently in his conflict with the Spirit, and his face was wet with tears.

'They are not torn down,' cried Scrooge, folding one of his bed-curtains in his arms, 'They are not torn down, rings and all. They are here—I am here—the shadows of the things that would have been may be dispelled. They will be. I know they will!'

His hands were busy with his garments all this time: turning them inside out, putting them on upside down, tearing them, mislaying them, making them parties to every kind of extravagance.

'I don't know what to do!' cried Scrooge, laughing and crying in the same breath, and making a perfect Laocoon of himself with his stockings. 'I am as light as a feather, I am as happy as an angel, I am as merry as a schoolboy, I am as giddy as a drunken man. A merry Christmas to everybody! A happy New Year to all the world! Hallo here! Whoop! Hallo!'

He had frisked into the sitting-room, and was now standing there, perfectly winded.

'There's the saucepan that the gruel was in!' cried Scrooge, starting off again, and going round the fireplace. 'There's the door by which the Ghost of Jacob Marley entered! There's the corner where the Ghost of Christmas Present sat! There's the window where I saw the wandering Spirits! It's all right, it's all true, it all happened. Ha, ha, ha!'

Really, for a man who had been out of practice for so many years, it was a splendid laugh, a most illustrious laugh. The father of a long, long line of brilliant laughs!

'I don't know what day of the month it is,' said Scrooge. 'I don't know how long I have been among the Spirits. I don't know anything. I'm quite a baby. Never mind. I don't care. I'd rather be a baby. Hallo! Whoop! Hallo here!'

He was checked in his transports by the churches ringing out the lustiest peals he had ever heard. Clash, clash, hammer; ding, dong, bell! Bell, dong, ding; hammer, clash, clash! Oh, glorious, glorious!

Running to the window, he opened it, and put out his head. No fog, no mist; clear, bright, jovial, stirring, cold; cold, piping for the blood to dance to; golden sunlight; heavenly sky; sweet fresh air; merry bells. Oh, glorious! Glorious!

'What's to-day?' cried Scrooge, calling downward to a boy in Sunday clothes, who perhaps had loitered in to look about him.

'EH?' returned the boy with all his might of wonder.

'What's to-day, my fine fellow?' said Scrooge.

'To-day!' replied the boy. 'Why, CHRISTMAS DAY.'

'It's Christmas Day!' said Scrooge to himself. 'I haven't missed it. The Spirits have done it all in one night. They can do anything they like. Of course they can. Of course they can. Hallo, my fine fellow!'

'Hallo!' returned the boy.

'Do you know the poulterer's in the next street but one, at the corner?' Scrooge inquired.

'I should hope I did,' replied the lad.

'An intelligent boy!' said Scrooge. 'A remarkable boy! Do you know whether they've sold the prize turkey that was hanging up there?—Not the little prize turkey: the big one?'

'What! the one as big as me?' returned the boy.

'What a delightful boy!' said Scrooge. 'It's a pleasure to talk to him. Yes, my buck!'

'It's hanging there now,' replied the boy.

'Is it?' said Scrooge. 'Go and buy it.'

'Walk-ER!' exclaimed the boy.

'No, no,' said Scrooge. 'I am in earnest. Go and buy it, and tell 'em to bring it here, that I may give them the directions where to take it. Come back with the man, and I'll give you a shilling. Come back with him in less than five minutes, and I'll give you half-a-crown!'

The boy was off like a shot. He must have had a steady hand at a trigger who could have got a shot off half as fast.

'I'll send it to Bob Cratchit's,' whispered Scrooge, rubbing his hands, and splitting with a laugh. 'He shan't know who sends it. It's twice the size of Tiny Tim. Joe Miller never made such a joke as sending it to Bob's will be!'

The hand in which he wrote the address was not a steady one; but write it he did, somehow, and went downstairs to open the street-door, ready for the coming of the poulterer's man. As he stood there, waiting his arrival, the knocker caught his eye.

'I shall love it as long as I live!' cried Scrooge, patting it with his hand. 'I scarcely ever looked at it before. What an honest expression it has in its face! It's a wonderful knocker! —Here's the turkey. Hallo! Whoop! How are you! Merry Christmas!'

It *was* a turkey! He never could have stood upon his legs, that bird. He would have snapped 'em short off in a minute, like sticks of sealing-wax.

'Why, it's impossible to carry that to Camden Town,' said Scrooge. 'You must have a cab.'

The chuckle with which he said this, and the chuckle with which he paid for the turkey, and the chuckle with which he paid for the cab, and the chuckle with which he recompensed the boy, were only to be exceeded by the chuckle with which he sat down breathless in his chair again, and chuckled till he cried.

Shaving was not an easy task, for his hand continued to shake very much; and shaving requires attention, even when you don't dance while you are at it. But if he had cut the end of his nose off, he would have put a piece of sticking-plaster over it, and been quite satisfied.

He dressed himself 'all in his best,' and at last got out into the streets. The people were by this time pouring forth, as he had seen them with the Ghost of Christmas Present; and, walking with his hands behind him, Scrooge regarded every one with a delighted smile. He looked so irresistibly pleasant, in a word, that three or four good-humoured fellows said, 'Good-morning, sir! A merry Christmas to you!' And Scrooge said often afterwards that, of all the blithe sounds he had ever heard, those were the blithest in his ears.

He had not gone far when, coming on towards him, he beheld the portly gentleman who had walked into his counting-house the day before, and said, 'Scrooge and Marley's, I believe?' It sent a pang across his heart to think how this old gentleman would look upon him when they met; but he knew what path lay straight before him, and he took it.

'My dear sir,' said Scrooge, quickening his pace, and taking the old gentleman by both his hands, 'how do you do? I hope you succeeded yesterday. It was very kind of you. A merry Christmas to you, sir!'

'Mr. Scrooge?'

'Yes,' said Scrooge. 'That is my name, and I fear it may not be pleasant to you. Allow me to ask your pardon. And will you have the goodness——' Here Scrooge whispered in his ear.

'Lord bless me!' cried the gentleman, as if his breath were taken away. 'My dear Mr. Scrooge, are you serious?'

'If you please,' said Scrooge. 'Not a farthing less. A great many back-payments are included in it, I assure you. Will you do me that favour?'

'My dear sir,' said the other, shaking hands with him, 'I don't know what to say to such munifi——'

'Don't say anything, please,' retorted Scrooge. 'Come and see me. Will you come and see me?'

'I will!' cried the old gentleman. And it was clear he meant to do it.

'Thankee,' said Scrooge. 'I am much obliged to you. I thank you fifty times. Bless you!'

He went to church, and walked about the streets, and watched the people hurrying to and fro, and patted the children on the head, and questioned beggars, and looked down into the kitchens of houses, and up to the windows; and found that everything could yield him pleasure. He had never dreamed that any walk—that anything—could give him so much happiness. In the afternoon he turned his steps towards his nephew's house.

He passed the door a dozen times before he had the courage to go up and knock. But he made a dash and did it.

'Is your master at home, my dear?' said Scrooge to the girl. 'Nice girl! Very.'

'Yes, sir.'

'Where is he, my love?' said Scrooge.

'He's in the dining-room, sir, along with mistress. I'll show you upstairs, if you please.'

'Thankee. He knows me,' said Scrooge, with his hand already on the dining-room lock. 'I'll go in here, my dear.'

He turned it gently, and sidled his face in round the door. They were looking at the table (which was spread out in great array); for these young housekeepers are always nervous on such points, and like to see that everything is right.

'Fred!' said Scrooge.

Dear heart alive, how his niece by marriage started! Scrooge had forgotten, for the moment, about her sitting in the corner with the footstool, or he wouldn't have done it on any account.

'Why, bless my soul!' cried Fred, 'who's that?'

'It's I. Your uncle Scrooge. I have come to dinner. Will you let me in, Fred?'

Let him in! It is a mercy he didn't shake his arm off. He was at home in five minutes. Nothing could be heartier. His niece looked just the same. So did Topper when *he* came. So did the plump sister when *she* came. So did every one when *they* came. Wonderful party, wonderful games, wonderful unanimity, won-der-ful happiness!

But he was early at the office next morning. Oh, he was early there! If he could only be there first, and catch Bob Cratchit coming late! That was the thing he had set his heart upon.

And he did it; yes, he did! The clock struck nine. No Bob. A quarter past. No Bob. He was full eighteen minutes and a half behind his time. Scrooge sat with his door wide open, that he might see him come into the tank.

His hat was off before he opened the door; his comforter too. He was on his stool in a jiffy, driving away with his pen, as if he were trying to overtake nine o'clock.

'Hallo!' growled Scrooge in his accustomed voice as near as he could feign it. 'What do you mean by coming here at this time of day?'

'I am very sorry, sir,' said Bob. 'I *am* behind my time.'

'You are!' repeated Scrooge. 'Yes, I think you are. Step this way, sir, if you please.'

'It's only once a year, sir,' pleaded Bob, appearing from the tank. 'It shall not be repeated. I was making rather merry yesterday, sir.'

'Now, I'll tell you what, my friend,' said Scrooge. 'I am not going to stand this sort of thing any longer. And there-fore,' he continued, leaping from his stool, and giving Bob such a dig in the waistcoat that he staggered back into the tank again—'and therefore I am about to raise your salary!'

Bob trembled, and got a little nearer to the ruler. He had a momentary idea of knocking Scrooge down with it, holding him, and calling to the people in the court for help and a strait-waistcoat.

'A merry Christmas, Bob!' said Scrooge, with an earnestness that could not be mistaken, as he clapped him on the back. 'A merrier Christmas, Bob, my good fellow, than I have given you for many a year! I'll raise your salary, and endeavour to assist your struggling family, and we will discuss your affairs this very afternoon, over a Christmas bowl of smoking bishop, Bob! Make up the fires and buy another coal-scuttle before you dot another i, Bob Cratchit!'

Scrooge was better than his word. He did it all, and infinitely more; and to Tiny Tim, who did NOT die, he was a second father. He became as good a friend, as good a master, and as good a man as the good old City knew, or any other good old city, town, or borough in the good old world. Some people laughed to see the alteration in him, but he let them laugh, and little heeded them; for he was wise enough to know that nothing ever happened on this globe, for good, at which some people did not have their fill of laughter in the outset; and knowing that such as these would be blind anyway, he thought it quite as well that they should wrinkle up their eyes in grins as have the malady in less attractive forms. His own heart laughed, and that was quite enough for him.

He had no further intercourse with Spirits, but lived upon the Total-Abstinence Principle ever afterwards; and it was always said of him that he knew how to keep Christmas well, if any man alive possessed the knowledge. May that be truly said of us, and all of us! And so, as Tiny Tim observed, God bless Us, Every One!

# ABOUT THE AUTHORS

**Kevin J. Anderson** has published more than 170 books, 58 of which have been national or international bestsellers. He has written numerous novels in the Star Wars, X-Files, and Dune universes, as well as unique steampunk fantasy novels *Clockwork Angels* and *Clockwork Lives*, written with legendary rock drummer Neil Peart. His original works include the Saga of Seven Suns series, the Wake the Dragon and Terra Incognita fantasy trilogies, the Saga of Shadows trilogy, and his humorous horror series featuring Dan Shamble, Zombie PI. He has edited numerous anthologies, written comics and games, and the lyrics to two rock CDs. Anderson is the director of the graduate program in Publishing at Western Colorado University. Anderson and his wife Rebecca Moesta are the publishers of WordFire Press. His most recent novels are *Vengewar, Dune: The Duke of Caladan* (with Brian Herbert), *Stake, Kill Zone* (with Doug Beason), *and Spine of the Dragon.*

**Charles Dickens** was a prolific British novelist, journalist, editor, illustrator, and social commentator who wrote such beloved classic novels as *Oliver Twist*, *A Christmas Carol*, *Nicholas Nickleby*, *David Copperfield*, *A Tale of Two Cities*, and *Great Expectations*.

Dickens is remembered as one of the most important, beloved, and influential writers of the 19th century. Among his accomplishments, he has been lauded for providing a stark portrait of the Victorian-era underclass, helping to bring about social change.

# ABOUT THE ILLUSTRATOR

**John Leech** (29 August 1817 –
29 October 1864) was a British
caricaturist and illustrator. He
was best known for his work for
Punch, a humorous magazine of
political satire with light social
comedy.

Leech was the first illustrator
of Charles Dickens' 1843 novella
A Christmas Carol. He was
furthermore a pioneer in comics,
creating the recurring character *Mr. Briggs* and some sequen-
tial illustrated gags.

*Worldbuilding: From Small Towns to Entire Universes*
*Writing As a Team Sport*
*On Being a Dictator*

*Mr. Wells & the Martians*

*Resurrection, Inc.*

*The Saga of Seven Suns, Veiled Alliances*
*The Saga of Seven Suns, Whistling Past the Graveyard*
*The Saga of Seven Suns: TWO SHORT NOVELS: Includes Veiled
Alliances and Whistling Past the Graveyard*
*Three Military SF Novellas*

**Short Story Collections**
*Selected Stories: Science Fiction, Volume 1*
*Selected Stories: Science Fiction, Volume 2*
*Selected Stories: Fantasy*
*Selected Stories: Horror and Dark Fantasy*

**By Kevin J. Anderson & Doug Beason**
*Assemblers of Infinity*
*Craig Kreident #1: Virtual Destruction*
*Craig Kreident #2: Fallout*
*Craig Kreident #3: Lethal Exposure*
*Ignition*
*Ill Wind*
*Lifeline*
*The Trinity Paradox*

**By Kevin J. Anderson & Rebecca Moesta**
*Collaborators*

*Crystal Doors #1: Island Realm*
*Crystal Doors #2: Ocean Realm*
*Crystal Doors #3: Sky Realm*
*Star Challengers #1: Moonbase Crisis*
*Star Challengers #2: Space Station Crisis*
*Star Challengers #3: Asteroid Crisis*

**Kevin J. Anderson & Neil Peart**
*Clockwork Angels*
*Clockwork Lives*
*Drumbeats*

Our list of other WordFire Press authors and titles is always growing. To find out more and to shop our selection of titles, visit us at:
wordfirepress.com

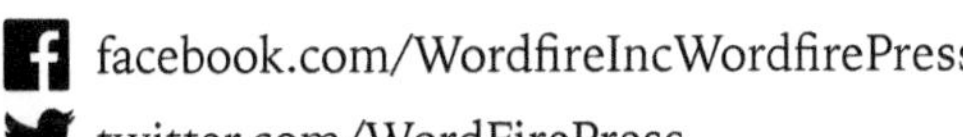

facebook.com/WordfireIncWordfirePress
twitter.com/WordFirePress
instagram.com/WordFirePress
bookbub.com/profile/4109784512